SKIN

BY TIMOTHY HARGREAVES

WILLOWS WEST

The characters and events portrayed in this book are fictitious. Any similarity to real persons, living or dead, is coincidental and not intended by the author.

ISBN: 979-8-9998695-5-5

Printed in the United States of America

For my first readers
Jo and Faye

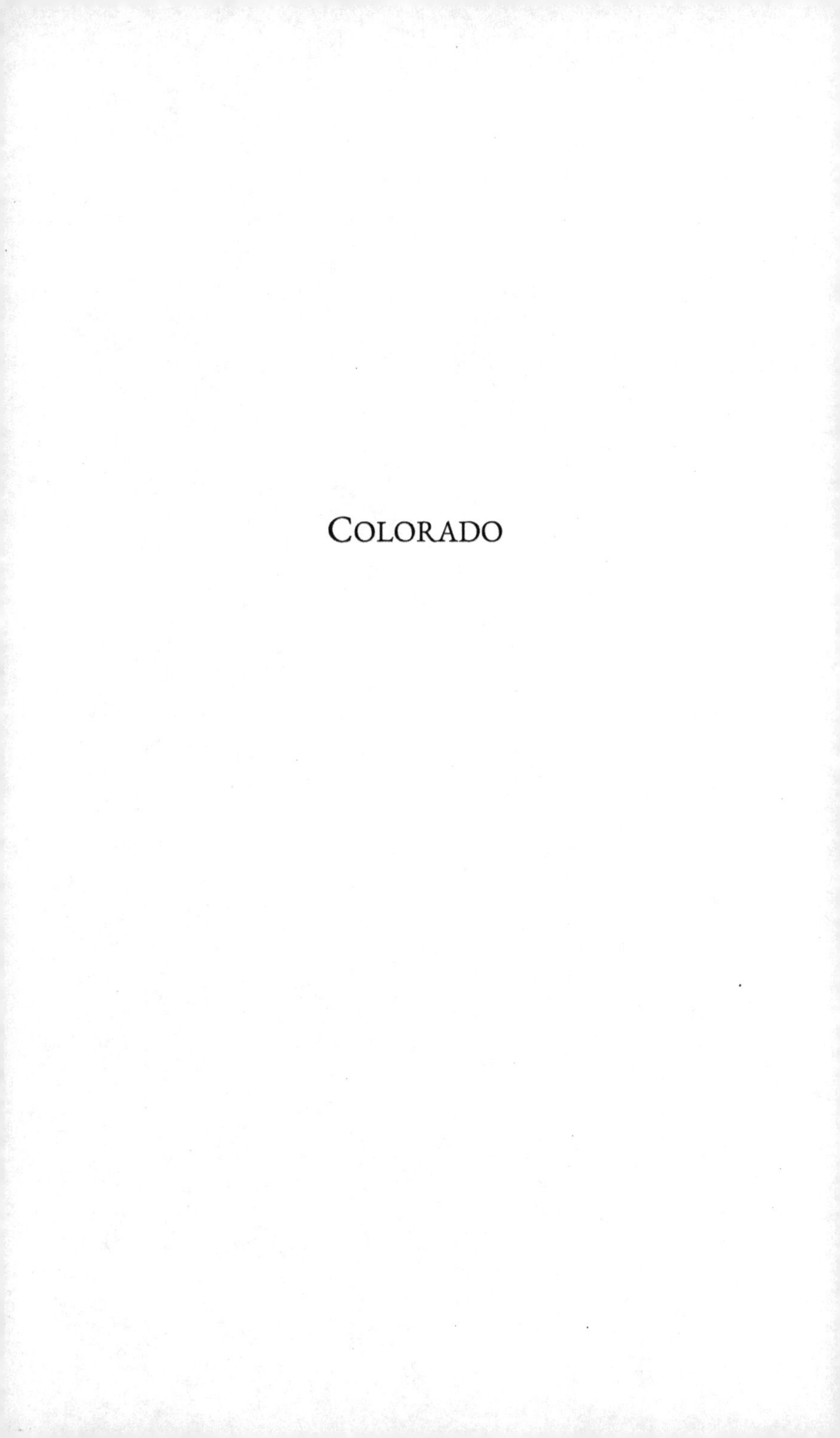

Colorado

One

IT BEGAN IN SUNLIGHT.

The long, golden kind that soaked the Kansas fields in late summer. Cicadas droned like old machines. Dust rose behind the bikes as they rattled down the dirt track, a tight pack of boys pedaling hard and reckless.

He was twelve or so. Summer vacation, and everything was wide and flat and full of daring. They shouldn't have been there. This was private land, and they knew it. But the hay barn called them, and they'd been before. The farmer hadn't caught them yet.

They ditched their bikes in the grass and ran, laughing, ducking into the cool gloom of the barn. It smelled of cut grass and animal droppings—stacked hay bales towered high. They got to work shifting, rearranging, setting out tunnels and dens. They shouted and crawled and scratched their arms. It was freedom, rough and breathless.

Later, they lay outside in a circle, backs in the grass, the sky wide overhead. The sun, high and hot. They talked about nothing and everything. The smell of warm hay clung to their clothes. Ladybugs were everywhere, dozens of them, crawling over their arms and faces, landing and lifting again. Tiny red sparks with black spots.

Then a boy sat up, picked a ladybug off his t-shirt, and held it gently in the palm of his hand. Next moment he pulled off a wing. He grabbed another and pulled off the back legs. Why would he do that? Another boy laughed and pulled out a lighter, flicked it once and torched five insects in one blast of his mini-flame thrower.

The others were quiet at first. Watching. Then two of them laughed. One joined in. Then another.

A small pile of blackened husks grew in the grass between them.

He couldn't move.

He felt alone, completely solitary among the gang of boys.

His body was heavy with it—disgust, shame and something older. He wanted to scream, or grab the lighter, or run. But he didn't. He sat there, sweating in hayfield, his heart hammering, while the crackle of small burning bodies filled his ears.

Two

DAN SAT UP IN BED, breathing hard, damp sheets twisted around his legs. The room was still dark, the corners blurry in the early light. Shankley was curled on the floor beside the bed, head raised, watching him with quiet concern. Dan pressed the heels of his hands into his eyes until the dream thinned and faded, leaving behind only the ache in his chest. He got up without a sound, pulled on yesterday's clothes, and reached for the leash, though he knew he wouldn't use it. Shankley was already standing, tail low, ready. They stepped outside into the hush of morning, the door clicking shut behind them.

He walked slowly, hands deep in the pockets of his canvas jacket, breath clouding in the cold air. A thin mist hanging low over the hills, softening the lines of the trees and muting the world into silence. Somewhere behind them, the town of Redcliff still slept, tucked in under frosted roofs and the long shadows of the mountains.

Shankley trotted ahead, nose to the ground, tail moving with the rhythm of some private investigation. The mutt's thick coat was already wet from the morning grass, and beads of moisture clung to his whiskers.

Dan's mind was elsewhere, caught on things he didn't care to name. Things he hadn't said to Allison. Things he wouldn't.

Shankley veered off toward a cluster of low spruce trees just beyond the trail. Dan slowed, not thinking much of it, until the stillness shattered.

A rush of wings broke from the underbrush. A pair of grouse exploded into the air, heavy and fast, their feathers slicing through the silence. They flew low, angling for deeper cover beyond the mist, their sudden violence gone almost as quickly as it had come.

Dan stopped dead. His heart racing.

Shankley stood alert, tail stiff, ears perked. Waiting for a look from Dan to confirm his outstanding work. The world seemed to hold its breath again.

Dan blinked into the quiet that followed, everything suddenly sharper, the cold in his lungs, the smell of wet earth, the fine tremble of a single branch still swaying from the birds' escape.

"Christ," he muttered, rubbing the back of his neck. "Okay. I'm awake."

Shankley gave a little huff and trotted back toward him, satisfied.

They walked on, the trail bending back toward the edge of town where the mist was beginning to lift. The rooftops of Redcliff emerged like islands, pale and still. A few porch lights glowed faintly. A solitary chimney was already puffing smoke into the damp morning air.

Dan kept his eyes on the path. Shankley, still energized from flushing the birds, trotted ahead in loose loops.

Their house sat near the edge of town, a squat two-bedroom rental with cracked siding and a porch that creaked with every step. The yard was mostly scrub grass and dirt, bordered by an old fence that couldn't decide if it was falling down or standing up. Dan liked that about it. It didn't pretend to be more than it was.

He stamped his boots on the steps and opened the door.

Inside, the warmth washed over him. The smell of coffee—strong, burnt, and familiar.

Allison stood at the kitchen counter, pouring over something on her tablet, a pen clutched absently in her left hand. Her hair was tied up messily, a few strands fallen loose.

"Hey," Dan said, shrugging off his jacket. "A stupid grouse nearly gave me a heart attack."

"That'll teach you to go wandering off in the fog," she said without looking up. Her voice was even, but held something Dan couldn't quite grasp. "The coffee just brewed if you want some?"

Dan poured a mug, leaning against the counter. Shankley curled onto his bed with a sigh, as if done for the day.

"How'd you sleep?" he asked after a moment.

"Okay."

Dan nodded. Let the silence settle between them.

Outside, the mist was beginning to break apart, sunlight threading its way through. He stared out the window, watching it. Something had shifted in him out there this morning, but it slipped away the moment he tried to name it.

"Allison," he said softly.

She looked up then, the pen pausing mid-air.

But whatever he'd meant to say was gone.

He took a sip of coffee instead.

Allison watched him, the steam curling past his face in the kitchen light. He looked like a man still halfway in a dream—silent, slow-moving. His eyes stayed fixed on something beyond the window, and she doubted he was seeing the yard. The room felt tighter when he was like this. Like everything and everyone had to tiptoe around whatever thought he was holding.

"I've got that inventory shift today," she said lightly, tapping her pen against the tablet. "Ben's out sick again. So it'll be me and Kelsey unloading everything from that delayed shipment. Ten crates, minimum. And guess who gets to reorganize the climbing section?"

Dan gave a small nod. "Mm."

She waited, watching for him to turn or ask or smile. He didn't.

She sighed evenly and flipped the pen through her fingers. "It'll be fine. Just a long day. I'll probably be home late."

Dan made a noncommittal noise, a half breath, half grunt. She watched the side of his face: still, unreadable.

Shankley stirred on the floor, wagged his tail once, then settled again.

Allison pushed her tablet aside and leaned on the counter. "You're not even here, are you?"

Dan blinked. Turned slightly. "What?"

"Nothing," she said, a little too fast. "Just talking to myself."

He looked at her properly then, brow creased like he was trying to catch up to the moment. "Sorry. I'm just tired."

She nodded. "Sure."

She kept the thought to herself—tired for months, I miss you, do you even notice when I leave.

Instead, she reached for her coffee, blew across the top, and took a sip. It was already cooling. Bitterness clung to the roof of her mouth.

Dan looked back to the window.

She watched him for another moment, then turned away. Opened the cupboard. Pulled out her lunch container and started packing her bag like she was doing it for the first time or the thousandth, it didn't matter.

Behind her, the silence hardened. Not hostile. Just... full of all the things neither of them had said in a long time.

"Allison," he said suddenly.

Her hand paused on the zipper. "Yeah?"

"I'll see you tonight."

She zipped the bag. Slung it over her shoulder.

"Alright Dan," she said.

He nodded. That same small, distant nod. Like it took effort just to stay on the surface of the world.

Dan checked the front door, turning the deadbolt out of habit. The house was quiet. A quiet that came when something had left. No footsteps on the stairs, no cupboard doors opening, no low hum of her voice from the other room. Just the soft creak of timber and the steady thump of Shankley's tail as he climbed onto the couch, curled into a tight crescent, and let out a long, satisfied sigh.

Dan stood there a moment, staring at the spot where her coat had hung.

His phone buzzed on the counter.

"Good morning, Martinez," he answered, recognizing his boss's mobile number.

Ken's voice was all business. "Remember, today's the day for that school visit. Don't forget to take some of the bear education stuff up to Kremmling with you. Middle school awareness day, definitely in your wheelhouse."

"I'll take the river road?"

"Sure, it should be open. Can you keep an eye out for birds of prey? Especially between State Bridge and Radium. See if any nests are getting rebuilt, maybe early returns. I want eyes on it."

Dan scratched absently at his chin. "Got it."

"No need to rush, but don't make a holiday out of it. Text me photos if you see anything interesting."

Click.

Dan set the phone down and looked at Shankley, now upside down on the couch, one paw flopped over his snout. "Hope you weren't planning to nap all day."

The dog's eyes opened lazily, then closed again.

They cut west out of Redcliff, wound through the canyon to Wolcott, then climbed onto 131, heading north. It was a familiar stretch, rolling scrubland, empty fences, low winter growth holding tight to the earth. He spotted a couple of horses standing stock still in a distant field like a couple of forgotten statues. The light was pale and clean, the sky wide open.

Shankley sat alert in the passenger seat, nose twitching at every roadside drift of scent that made it through the cracked window. Somewhere up ahead, the river waited.

Near State Bridge, the land dropped gently into the cut where the Colorado first showed its face, fast and brown with early melt. Dan slowed and pulled into a gravel turnout. He grabbed binoculars from the glovebox and stepped out into the still cold air. The river moved with a slow urgency, pushing around rocks that jutted like bones through the surface.

Up on the far side, there was a large nest. Sticks and bleached grass woven high in the crown of a dead tree. He steadied the binoculars and there she was, an osprey. Perched on the rim, feathers ruffling in the breeze, sharp eyes scanning the water.

Dan stayed there for a while, watching. The bird didn't move. Just held its place like it had always been there, like it always would be.

Back in the truck, Shankley rested his head on Dan's knee as they pulled away.

Something eased in Dan's chest. The silence still felt like absence, but out here, it wasn't empty. There was space. Room to breathe.

A few miles past State Bridge, Dan took the turnoff toward Radium. The dirt road curled away from the River Road and began its slow descent through sagebrush flats and dry, wind-cut gullies. He downshifted, letting the truck idle low as it rolled over washboards and shallow ruts. It wasn't scenic in the traditional sense—closed in, a fence line that had given up long ago—but it held something for him. Familiar terrain. A kind of pause.

He checked the clock, still ahead of schedule for Kremmling. The detour was unplanned, but he didn't question it.

The river didn't come into view until the final bend. One last drop and there it was, broad and swollen with early melt, sliding cold and brown between low canyon walls. He pulled into a flat clearing near the bluff and killed the engine.

Down below, tucked in behind a screen of willows was the hot spring. He couldn't see the steam from here, but he knew it was there, rising faintly from the rocks where it always had. He and Allison had come out a few times. Usually in spring. Waded across barefoot, half-shivering, laughing, balancing on river stones slick with moss. She used to lean back against the edge, steam in her hair, eyes closed like nothing in the world could touch her.

Dan stayed in the cab.

Shankley nosed the window and gave a low chuff. In the dry grass near the trailhead, a pair of marmots bounced over a sunlit patch, thick with winter fur and hungry-looking. A flicker worked at a nearby cottonwood, carving out its season's claim with sharp, echoing strikes. Somewhere in the background, the river kept moving.

Dan watched the scene. He didn't feel like going down. But he was glad he'd stopped.

Eventually, he turned the key and shifted back into drive. The road climbed behind him, leaving the river to its work.

Kremling Middle School was a low, sprawling building set just back from the highway, its parking lot still patched with snow. Dan pulled in and parked by a line of pickups, glanced at the clock—ten minutes early—and killed the engine.

Inside the cab, Shankley gave a low whine, sensing the stop.

"Stay here, boy," Dan said, scratching behind the dog's ear. "This one's all mine."

He grabbed the duffel with the bear awareness materials—models, track casts, a laminated poster of a black bear in mid-stride—and headed toward the front entrance.

The school smelled like pencil shavings, hand sanitizer, and cafeteria grease. A secretary walked him through to the multipurpose room, where folding chairs had been arranged in loose rows and a projector hummed softly near the back.

A teacher in a forest-green fleece met him with a grateful handshake. "Thanks for coming, Mr. Nowak. I wasn't sure if anyone would be able to make the trip this early in the season."

"Call me Dan. And yeah, roads are clear enough. Good excuse to check on the ospreys."

The woman smiled. "Let me know if you need anything. We've got about thirty kids coming in—fifth and sixth grade."

Dan set up near the front. He unzipped the duffel, laid out rubber paw prints and jars labeled *bear scent, male and female,* and clipped the poster to a portable easel. As the students trickled in, he felt himself straighten—the quiet recalibration he'd done a hundred times. An internal rebalancing. He stood a little straighter. Found his rhythm.

"Alright," he said once the room had settled. "Let's talk bears."

He didn't talk down to them. That was the trick. You gave them real knowledge, let them ask the weird questions, and never faked a story. He passed around the rubber tracks, let them sniff the scent jars if they were brave enough. Got them to guess which paw was front and which was back. He talked scat, food sources, and denning behavior. A kid in a Broncos hoodie asked if bears ever chased after people, and Dan explained how rare it was, how most incidents came from surprise or carelessness.

He moved easily through it, engaged and professional. Even cracked a joke or two.

And as he watched their faces shift from skeptical to curious, he felt, just for a little while, like the world was something he could still explain. Something that made sense.

Afterward, the teacher thanked him again and offered a cafeteria coffee. He declined politely, packed up his gear, and stepped back out into the wind.

In the truck, Shankley lifted his head in greeting. Dan rubbed the dog's neck and sat for a moment, staring out at the mountains beyond town. The day was still open in front of him, but it felt tighter now, like something had closed behind him. Not in a bad way. Just... finished.

He turned the key, checked the mirror, and pulled out onto the road.

The phone buzzed in the console. Ken.

Dan tapped the hands-free. "Yeah?"

"Hey. How'd it go?" Ken's voice was always louder than necessary, even through the truck's speakers.

"Fine. They were sixth graders. They mostly wanted to know if I'd ever tranquilized a mountain lion."

Ken laughed. "Did you tell them about the one in Basalt that ran up the stairwell?"

"No," Dan said. "Didn't want to give them ideas."

"Well, speaking of wild animals..." Ken cleared his throat. "Need you to swing by Wolford on the way back. One of the fisheries guys flagged something—says it might be mussel activity. Could be nothing, but it needs to be checked."

"Copy that. Anyone meeting me there?"

"Negative. It's probably a false alarm, but we need to log it either way."

Dan nodded, adjusting his grip on the wheel. "I'll take a look."

"One more thing," Ken added. "Tomorrow morning—we've got a wolf reintroduction update at HQ. There's a couple of state folks coming in. I'd like you in the room."

Dan hesitated. "Okay. That's short notice."

"Yeah, I know. I was going to wait, but the list changed this morning. Bring Allison if she's around. Meeting in the morning, then take her to the hot springs after. She likes those, right?"

Dan glanced at Shankley in the rearview. The dog had sprawled across the back seat again, nose twitching in sleep.

"Yeah," Dan said. "She does."

"Good. The meeting's scheduled for nine. We'll keep it under two hours."

"Sounds good."

"Appreciate it," Ken said. "Let me know what you find at Wolford."

The call ended, and the truck settled back into silence.

Dan took the turn toward the reservoir, the asphalt opening up ahead of him.

There were no mussels at Wolford. Just a pair of bored rangers at the boat ramp, wind pushing ripples across the reservoir, and the faint tang of gasoline near the docks. Dan made a sweep along the shoreline anyway, took a few photos, logged the coordinates, and left the file open for Ken with a short note: "No evidence of infestation. No boats launched in last 72 hrs."

Now, heading south again, the sun was lower and the light had turned golden, throwing long shadows across the road. Shankley's nose was pressed to the rear window, ears flicking at every roadside movement.

The quiet was welcome.

The road curved gently west, paralleling the Colorado River. Cottonwoods still stood bare, but buds had begun to swell at the branch tips—those tight little fists of green promise. Red rock cliffs flared up in places where the land had been cleaved open, and the river moved with a kind of muscular grace beside it all, unconcerned.

Dan drove with the window cracked. Spring air poured in, cool and full of dust and water and sun-warmed bark. It smelled like waking things.

Somewhere in the trees, a crow called out—sharp and confident, as if it had something important to announce.

Dan glanced up just in time to see a dark shape lift from the riverbank and wheel across the canyon wall, wings catching the late light.

He didn't know why, but the sight of it gave him a chill—not fear exactly, but a strange pulse of alertness, like something in him had leaned forward to listen.

He shifted in his seat and shook it off.

Just a bird.

Dan dropped down the winding road into Redcliff just as the last of the sun brushed the ridge.

The town unfolded below like a secret someone had forgotten to tell the rest of the world. Tucked into a tight mountain canyon, Redcliff clung to the hillside with a kind of stubborn charm—half-wild, half-remembered. The buildings were mismatched and weathered, a scattered collection of cabins, old miner's homes, and century-old frame houses set at odd angles to the road. Most had metal roofs and patched siding. A few were painted bright blues or reds that had long since faded to something softer. Earth tones by default.

Redcliff had been the county seat back in the late 1800's, before the silver crash. You could still see the bones of that ambition—stone foundations half-swallowed by earth, rusted rail cars tucked along the river, a collapsed bridge that had once carried ore and men out of the canyon.

The residents fit the place, off-grid types, lifers, and artists with day jobs. Ski techs who preferred solitude over pay. A handful of older locals who remembered when the post office was the only heated building in town. Nobody put on airs in Redcliff. You didn't last long here if you needed more than a woodstove and some privacy.

Dan turned onto his street, gravel popping under the tires. Their house was a rental, it had good bones, low eaves, and a view of the cliffs if you stood at a certain angle.

He parked in the shadow of the porch and shut off the engine. Shankley stirred and stood, tail wagging. Dan let him lick his hand, then moved out into the stillness.

Somewhere in the distance, a dog barked once and fell silent.

Dan stepped inside and closed the door behind him. The air was warm and smelled faintly of woodsmoke and curry. He toed off his boots and hung his jacket by the door.

From the kitchen, Allison called, "I thought I'd be the last one home tonight."

He smiled and followed the sound of her voice. She was barefoot, standing at the stove, already out of her work things, stirring something in a cast iron pan. Her hair was loose, and there was a glass of wine half full on the counter.

"Yeah, Ken called and sent me to check something at Wolford but it ended up being a false alarm" Dan said.

"Glad to hear it." She turned down the burner and gave him a quick kiss on the cheek. "Hungry?"

"Starving."

She plated up two bowls without fuss—lentils, rice, some kind of roasted squash—and handed one to him with a fork already in it. They moved to the couch like they'd done a hundred times before, Shankley settling at their feet.

"Oh, Ken wants me in Glenwood tomorrow morning," Dan said between bites. "There's a wolf reintroduction update. Some folks from the state are coming in."

She raised her eyebrows. "Sounds exciting."

"Maybe. He said to bring you, if you're free. The meeting's in the morning and he suggested we hit the hot springs after."

Allison took a sip of wine and nodded. "I'm off tomorrow. That actually sounds great."

Dan leaned back, the warmth of the food settling in his chest. "Could be nice."

They ate quietly for a while, bowls balanced on their knees, the room lit by the amber glow of a single lamp in the corner. Outside, night closed around the town.

No plans, no pressure. Just the simple peace of two people finishing their day, side by side.

Outside, the stars started to show above the ridge, faint and watchful, impassive to the slow revolution of the world below.

THREE

THEY PULLED OFF the interstate just after eight-thirty, merging into the low gear rhythm of morning traffic. Work trucks, wagons with ski racks, county vehicles—all edging through town in quiet procession. Glenwood was fully awake now, its streets filled with people already mid-routine: coffee in hand, earbuds in, faces set toward the day.

Dan guided the truck off Grand Avenue and down a side street, past a row of weathered storefronts and angled brick facades. Between the hardware store and old hotels, newer signs had crept in—boutique this, organic that—but the bones of the town held strong. Glenwood hadn't let go of itself entirely.

"There's an outdoor shop a couple blocks from here," Dan said, his eyes flicking to the sidewalk. "Might be worth checking out while I'm in the meeting."

Allison gave a small nod, brushing a hand through her hair. "Sure. I'll find it."

"And if you're up for a walk, Doc Holliday's grave is up the hill. Good view from the top."

She glanced over at him, not unkindly. "I'll see how I feel."

Dan pulled into a metered spot near the state building and killed the engine. The heater ticked as it settled into stillness.

He looked over at her, hand still on the key. "My meeting shouldn't take long. I'll text when we wrap up."

"Okay." She reached for her coat, already halfway out the door.

She hesitated just a second, then looked back in. "Good luck with the update."

He nodded. "Have fun snooping on gear prices."

That got the hint of a smile, nothing more. She closed the door and turned up the street, shoulders tucked in slightly against the cold.

* * *

They met back near the truck around eleven-thirty. The street was busier now with lunch traffic, delivery vans, people passing with takeout in hand. Dan leaned against the passenger side door, arms crossed, watching a magpie hop along the power lines overhead.

Allison appeared from around the corner, sunglasses on, a paper bag tucked under one arm.

"How was your meeting?" she asked.

"Not bad. Mostly slides and recycled optimism."

She smiled. "Did you eat?"

"Yeah, it was definitely a government spread. Bagel and cream cheese, fruit and yogurt. I'm good."

She held up the bag. "Well, I'm starving."

They drove across town and parked near the Hot Springs. Steam rose in long ribbons from the surface of the pool, already half-full with families and retirees making the most of a weekday soak. The air had warmed just enough to smell faintly of sulfur and sun-warmed concrete.

"Did you know it was built in the 1880s," Dan said, more to fill space than inform. "Supposed to be the largest hot springs pool in the world."

Allison raised her brows, unimpressed. "That's a very Colorado thing to be proud of."

"Yeah."

Inside, they changed and met again poolside. Allison pulled on a swim cap and adjusted her goggles with the practiced movements of someone who needed motion. "I'm gonna get a few laps in," she said, already moving toward the lap lanes.

Dan nodded and stepped into the water of a soaking pool, letting it take him inch by inch.

He found a quiet spot and settled in, the heat soaking into his joints, loosening things he hadn't realized were tight. The noise of the pool blurred into a low wash—splashing, voices, laughter. None of it touched him.

He watched Allison glide past now and then—sharp and efficient, her rhythm unbroken. She didn't stop between lengths, flipping turns, then stroking back the other way.

Dan let himself drift, spine heavy and limbs suspended. The water held him—familiar, old, indifferent.

Eventually, Allison returned. She lowered herself beside him with a sigh, steam rising from her shoulders.

"Nice?" he asked.

She nodded. "It felt good to move."

They sat together without speaking, shoulders just brushing as the heat sank deeper.

They were on the road mid-afternoon, drifting back onto the interstate, windows cracked. The truck moved easily, coasting into the canyon's long sweep of walls and shadow. The road followed the river—winding and persistent.

Towering walls rose on either side, layered in rust and ochre, streaked with snowmelt that marked the passing of time. The Colorado River ran beside them, swollen with spring runoff, crashing and foaming around massive boulders. Ragged cottonwoods leaned in along the banks, their early buds flashing green.

Allison drove, her sunglasses reflecting the sky. She didn't speak. For now, the silence was easy.

The road curved again, pulling them east, deeper into the narrowing maw of the canyon. Every turn revealed a new cathedral: spires of rock, then sudden gaps of sky.

Birds wheeled above them—hawks maybe, or ravens—riding the thermals between stone and sun. Dan watched one spiral, then vanish.

As they passed Grizzly Creek, a flicker of motion caught his eye.

It came from the north, up the narrow slash of valley where the fire had burned two summers ago. The trees still stood, blackened and hollow.

Dan caught a flash, and he twisted in his seat to get a better view.

The angle of the light made it hard to see. Shadows fell across the slope like jagged tears, but something was there.

Not a shape exactly. A shift. A pulse of movement in the air, not quite natural. Like a wingbeat, or—

Gone.

He blinked, sat forward slightly. The world closing around him, the sound of the river louder against the glass.

"Everything alright?" Allison asked, eyes still on the road.

"Yeah," he said, voice quieter than he meant it to be. "Just... thought I saw something."

She didn't press him. The canyon bent again, hiding Grizzly Creek behind them.

But Dan kept looking back, long after it had disappeared.

Something itched in his chest as the canyon slipped past.

He watched the curve of the river, the flicker of light through bare branches, the shimmer where sun hit water. But it was in the background now. His focus was internal. Tight. Like a sound just at the edge of hearing, or a word on the verge of being spoken.

The feeling didn't pass, it expanded.

There was pressure behind his eyes, not painful, just unfamiliar. Like his body was adjusting to a space that no longer fit.

He blinked and the road doubled, just for a second. The colors of the canyon deepened, the red rock darkening as the river pulsed, gleaming like light on oil. The air inside the truck was thick with silence.

A shadow swept across the windshield.

Dan flinched and looked up but nothing was there.

"Dan, are you okay?" Allison asked again, glancing over.

He opened his mouth to answer—but the words didn't come. He couldn't hear the engine or the thrum of tires. Instead, he felt the wind. Cool, and high, and free.

He was moving. No—*flying*. The air rushed past his face—no, not his face, something sharper, smaller. A beak. A body light enough to ride the updraft, to tilt and dive, to skim just above the ragged tree line.

He wheeled once, turned again. Something clicked inside him. A door opening to a room that had always been there.

Below, the river spun like a broken mirror. Above, the cliffs reached for the sky and fell away.

He let out a sound—harsh, sharp, automatic.

A caw. A call.

And somewhere, unseen, another called back.

He blinked and the canyon snapped back around him like a closing door—sound, shape, weight. He was in the passenger seat again, legs stiff, fingers tingling where they rested on his thigh.

The truck was still moving. Allison was still driving.

She glanced at him, then back at the road. "You spaced out for a second."

Dan didn't answer right away. His heart was racing, but quietly, like something sprinting deep underground. He flexed his fingers, slowly. Everything felt too solid.

"Are you alright?" she asked.

"Yeah," he said, though it came out dry. "Yeah. Just... zoned out, I guess."

"You kind of froze. Just staring out the window. I thought you saw something."

"I don't know," he said. "Maybe I did."

She gave a small nod, her eyes focused ahead. The canyon opened up again, cliffs giving way to sky.

Dan sank a little lower in his seat. The pressure in his chest hadn't gone away, not entirely.

But now it was something else.

A memory forming at the edge of language.

Later, miles down the road, with Allison humming along to something low on the radio and the canyon behind them, Dan let the memory back in.

It came in pieces. Not as thought, but as sense.

The feeling of the wind under him, *not* against him. Lifting and shaping his path like a hand at the small of his back. The fine-tuned pressure of air along feathers he didn't have anymore but could still feel: primaries splayed to catch a rising current, tail angled for balance. Every twitch mattered.

The smell of the canyon had been different—sharper, simpler. Dust and sap and the dry metallic bite of rock warming in the sun. Even the river smelled faster.

And the sight—no longer a field of vision, but a *flood*. Everything in motion. Every glint, every dart of shadow, every subtle tremor of movement below, tracked and logged in perfect clarity. He had seen a beetle cross a log from fifty feet up. Remembering it hesitate at a gap in the bark.

And the others. The *murder*.

They had come into view all at once—half a dozen crows rising from the trees below, calling out in clipped bursts that weren't quite language, but close enough to stir something in him. A chorus of awareness. We see you. We're here. Join us or don't—but know that we are watching.

He remembered calling out in return—without thinking, without choosing. The sound had come from somewhere deep and ancient and automatic.

Then the shape of his body had cracked.

Not broken, just... split. Like a husk peeling back. And underneath it, something older. Something that had always been there, waiting its turn.

Dan sat still, breathing slowly through his nose, eyes half-focused on the road ahead. The memory didn't frighten him. Not yet.

But it felt more real than the canyon they'd left behind.

And far more permanent.

FOUR

TOM DELANEY STOOD BESIDE HIS CRUISER at the edge of the construction site, squinting uphill toward the half-built chalet. The morning sun was low, the pale light filtered through high cirrus. Meltwater ran in quiet trickles down the asphalt.

"Still in there?" he asked.

The security guy nodded. "He climbed in around dawn. Must have tipped the lid back himself—smart little bastard. He's been rooting around for an hour. I'd go closer, but..." He gestured vaguely toward the bear-sized problem.

Tom glanced at the dumpster—oversized, rust-rimmed, stationed close to the construction site. A dark shape shifted inside giving Tom his first look at the animal.

"It doesn't look full grown," Tom muttered.

He pulled out his phone and scrolled for Dan's number.

It rang twice before picking up. "Yeah?"

"Morning. Are you out and about?"

"Sort of," Dan said. "I'm parked down near the river. Checking on that eagle nest below the train bridge."

"Great, you're close. I've got a dumpster diver in Bachelor Gulch. Young black bear, not sure if it's tagged. It's at a construction site. Security's nervous, and I'd rather not escalate unless we have to."

Dan exhaled into the receiver. "Does he seem aggressive?"

"No. Just hungry. Calm for now, but it's only a matter of time before someone does something stupid."

Dan didn't hesitate. "I'll head up."

"Appreciate it."

Tom hung up and slipped the phone back into his pocket. He looked back at the dumpster, where a plastic bag flew up like a flag and dropped again.

"Help's on the way," he said quietly.

Dan turned off the gravel spur and let the truck idle for a second, eyes still on the eagle nest.

The bird was there, perched high in a gnarled cottonwood above the river, just visible through the tangle of branches. She hadn't moved since he parked. Still and regal, feathers dark against the brightening sky. Her mate was nowhere in sight.

He snapped a quick photo on his phone, logged the sighting with a brief note, then set the device aside and started the engine.

"Alright," he muttered to Shankley, who sat alert in the passenger seat. "Let's go deal with a spoiled teenager in a gated resort."

The road to Bachelor Gulch climbed fast and smooth, every curve carefully engineered, the asphalt fresh enough to gleam. Retaining walls made of hand-set stone lined the edges. Cut timbers framed custom street signs. Snowmelt ran neatly into grated drains.

He passed a trailhead kiosk with a cedar-shingled roof, then a row of tastefully spaced aspens lining the entrance road. At the gate, a uniformed security guard stepped halfway out of the booth, then gave a short wave as he recognized the truck. The arm barrier stayed down, but the side lane opened for him. If he'd been driving anything else, he'd have been stopped.

The homes here weren't just houses—they were statements. Multi-million-dollar retreats tucked behind landscaping sculpted with care to reflect nature now held at a distance. Wildlife was welcome only when it stayed at a distance.

Dan followed a new driveway marked *Construction Access Only*.

Tom stood at a distance, arms crossed, watching a large green dumpster like it might sprout wings.

Dan pulled in behind him, stepped out.

"Appreciate the assist," Tom said, offering a small nod. "The bear's still in there."

Dan walked forward slowly, eyes scanning the situation. The dumpster sat at the edge of the driveway, tilted slightly on the uneven gravel.

Tom gestured. "Security thought that he's untagged, but I couldn't confirm that. No collar, anyway."

Dan squinted at the shifting shadows inside. A rustle, a snort, then the bear's head appeared, young, sleek-coated, alert. He paused, ears twitching, then dropped back inside with a thunk and a soft crinkle of plastic.

"Juvenile for sure," Dan said. "Probably spring dispersal. Looking for an easy meal, not trouble."

He stepped quietly along the side of the dumpster, crouching near the rear bumper of a parked contractor's truck for a better look.

The bear surfaced again, nosing through a bag of leftovers. This time, Dan caught it, a glint of metal on the left ear, just below the tip.

"There," he said. "Tagged. Numbered. Left ear."

Tom's jaw tightened. "Shit, that's a second offense."

Dan nodded slowly. "That complicates it."

The bear sat back briefly, holding something between its paws, an intact breakfast burrito in wax paper.

Then he tore into it.

Dan didn't wait.

He moved back to the truck, grabbed the tranquilizer kit from the lockbox, and loaded a dart with smooth, practiced motion. Tom watched without speaking, just stepped aside to give him space.

"Are you sure?" he asked.

Dan nodded once. "He's small enough. Won't take much."

Tom gave a short nod, then turned to the nearby security officer. "Keep your people clear. This isn't a show."

Dan approached the dumpster slowly, circling to the open end. The bear was still inside, rustling around near the bottom, half-hidden by torn plastic and collapsed takeout boxes.

Dan raised the dart rifle, aimed for the muscle of the rear haunch, and fired.

The soft *phffft* of the dart was swallowed by the construction noise behind them. The bear grunted, twisted once, then staggered against the side of the bin. It scrabbled for balance, knocking over a shattered drywall bucket, then slumped with a groan.

They gave it five minutes.

With help from Tom, the site foreman, and one reluctant security guard, they hauled the bear out of the bin and into the back of Dan's rig, strapping it in with the field crate and a thick tarp.

Only after the bear was secured in the truck did Dan pull out his phone and call his boss.

It rang twice before Ken picked up. "Martinez."

"It's Dan. I've got a situation up at Bachelor Gulch. I got a call from the sheriff—a juvenile black bear got into a construction dumpster."

Ken's tone shifted, alert now. "Tagged?"

"Yeah. Left ear. No collar, but it's a state number."

"Did you sedate it?"

Dan hesitated, just long enough to answer the question. "Yeah. He's down and loaded. Still out cold."

A pause. "Dan..."

"He's calm. No signs of aggression. The dumpster was open, food waste everywhere. It's a second offense, but there's some mitigating circumstances."

"You know the policy."

"I've got a spot above Eagle," Dan said, already stepping away from the truck to put space between himself and the others. "Remote basin. No trash, no foot traffic. He gets one more shot."

"That's not how this works," Ken said. "You don't call me *after* the dart. That's not a discussion, it's a report."

"I made the call," Dan said. "He's a yearling, Ken. Still learning. This wasn't aggression—it was access."

Silence stretched between them. The only sound was wind curling through the pine above the site.

Finally, Ken exhaled. "You'd better be right."

"I understand."

The call ended. Dan stood for a moment with the phone still in his hand, the weight of the choice settling into his shoulders.

Then he turned back.

The construction foreman was waiting. He looked annoyed but cautious.

"That dumpster's a buffet," Dan said flatly. "That's on you."

The man raised a hand, half-defensive. "We've got lids. Someone must've left it open overnight."

"That's how this happens. One set of scraps, and a bear starts associating humans with food. Then it escalates. And we get the call."

He didn't raise his voice. He didn't have to.

The foreman looked away. "We'll tighten it up."

"Make sure you do. Next time might not be salvageable."

Dan turned, walking back to the truck. His jaw was tight, shoulders high.

Tom caught him before he climbed in.

"Hey," he said, hand on the door. "You did right."

Dan exhaled through his nose. "We'll see."

Tom smiled faintly. "Look—Kira and I wanted to have you guys over. Can't do this weekend but what about the following. You should come down and bring Allison. You could both use a free dinner."

Dan hesitated, then gave a small nod. "Yeah. That sounds good."

Tom patted the door. "I'll text you."

Dan climbed into the truck. In the back, the bear's chest rose and fell in steady rhythm. The tag on its ear caught the light once, then turned away.

He pulled out slowly, letting the tires roll quiet over the gravel, leaving the construction site behind.

* * *

The road narrowed to a rutted track, then disappeared altogether into a stand of fir and aspen. Dan parked just shy of the tree line and turned off the truck. The only sound was wind, high and dry, shifting the branches overhead.

He circled to the back of the truck, checked the bear's breathing one last time, then unlatched the crate.

"Easy," he murmured. "You've still got a world to wake up to."

The door creaked open.

Dan pulled down the tailgate of the truck. He had maneuvered to allow the bear the shortest drop he could. The incline wasn't gentle, but it would do.

He stepped back.

For a moment, nothing.

Then the bear stirred, groggy, and unsure. It blinked against the light, sniffed the air, and dragged itself forward, one paw scraping the metal crate floor. It hesitated at the edge of the tailgate, swayed, then made the short drop down to the pine duff with a thump and a grunt.

He paused there, unsteady.

Then another step. Then another.

His body remembered.

Dan stayed still.

The bear gave a low grunt, shook its head once, then ambled forward. Not fast. Not afraid. He moved slowly and steadily toward the ridge.

A minute later, he was gone—vanished into the trees like he'd never been caught at all.

Dan stood there a while longer, listening to the wind and the hush that followed.

FIVE

THE RIVER WAS RUNNING HIGH with spring melt. Whitewater thundered through the concrete drops at the kayak park, kicking spray into the late afternoon sun. A trio of kayakers waited their turn upstream, helmets glinting, paddles resting on their knees. One dropped in, angled bow-first into the hole, then disappeared in a burst of white, only to resurface seconds later downstream, arms pulling in clean strokes.

Dan and Allison walked the path above the bank. Ahead, Tom and Kira stood waiting near a weathered overlook rail, two drinks in hand.

"Hey, strangers," Tom called as they approached. "We thought you forgot."

Dan gave a wave. "We operate on Redcliff time now. That's like mountain standard plus distractions."

Tom handed him one of the drinks, a clear plastic cup with something citrusy and fizzing inside.

"Virgin mojitos, Tom said"

"Mocktails," Kira added. "Don't let him pretend he came up with that."

"Works for me," Dan said, taking a sip.

Allison smiled and accepted the second cup from Kira. "Boy, this river's loud."

"It's perfect," Tom said. "They added boulders last year. It made the eddy line cleaner, gives the kayakers better control through the second drop."

"You still kayak?" Dan asked.

Tom snorted. "Not since I pulled a rotator cuff helping some college kid out of a strainer."

They all laughed lightly and leaned into the rail. A breeze swept up from the water, cool and clean with river grit—air that left your skin feeling washed.

Another boat dropped in, a bright orange streak, and powered onto the standing wave with practiced rhythm.

"Not a bad way to spend an afternoon," Kira said.

"Sure beats another round of inventory," Allison added, sipping her drink.

They watched for a few moments, content.

Then Tom said, "You guys follow the latest on the wolf reintroduction?"

Dan didn't answer right away, tracking the next paddler. Young, lean, and a little shaky in the boat. He watched until the kid made it out upright.

"Some," he said. "Ken's keeping tabs. The State's trying to sound like it's all under control."

Tom shook his head. "This is what happens when city voters make mountain decisions."

Kira arched an eyebrow. "You mean democracy?"

Tom waved a hand. "Come on. Half of Boulder has never seen a cow in daylight. They vote yes on wolves because it sounds romantic. Meanwhile, ranchers are the ones who deal with the fallout."

Allison made a small noise of agreement. "I don't know. Seems like one of those things that sounds better than it plays out. Pretty on paper, but real messy in practice."

Dan took another sip of the mocktail, letting the mint muddle slowly on his tongue. "I get both sides," he said. "We need apex predators. But yeah, there's gonna be friction. People don't understand how wide an elk herd can roam."

"And they forget how tight a fence line can be," Tom added. "That's the problem. One dead calf and the whole valley will be up in arms."

Kira tilted her cup toward the river. "Or maybe we remember the land too late. The wolves aren't new. We're the last ones here."

No one spoke for a moment. Down in the eddy, a paddler tipped, rolled, and came back up again, water sheeting off the curve of their helmet.

They left the roar of the river behind and followed the sidewalk east, the town softening as they went. Traffic thinned. Storefronts gave way to aspens and low brick buildings, front porches and wind chimes. The air had lost any final tinge of winter this far down the valley, spring always came early to Eagle.

Kira walked beside Allison, gesturing toward a small garden tucked between two units—raised beds and early greens poking through.

"The garden's a community project," she said. "Tom claims he's allergic to kale, so I plant it out of spite."

Allison smiled. "That's a good policy."

Behind them, Dan walked with Tom, both hands in his jacket pockets.

"Do you really think they're ready for wolves?" Tom asked.

Dan shrugged. "They're ready on paper."

Tom gave a grunt. "On paper. Right."

They turned onto a quieter street. Across the way, a pair of kids tossed a frisbee on a patch of open grass, a golden retriever trying and failing to keep up with the plastic disc.

"I've got steaks," Kira said, glancing back at Allison, "and a roasted veggie plate for you, no mushrooms, right?"

"Perfect," Dan said. "Thanks for the invite."

"We've been meaning to do this for weeks," she replied. "Life just... keeps rolling."

Dan nodded, even though she wasn't looking.

Tom gestured toward a line of attached townhomes just ahead. "Ours is the one with the owl by the door."

Sure enough, a carved wooden owl perched on the entry post, eyes wide and unblinking. A little weathered, a little whimsical.

"Picked it up at a fair in Durango," Kira said as they stepped inside. "Tom said it was ugly. Now it guards the house."

"I've learned to pick my battles," Tom muttered.

Inside, the townhouse was modest and lived-in. A long bookshelf sagged under the weight of paperbacks, field guides, and a few framed photos of hiking trips. The kitchen was open, with scuffed tile and mismatched mugs drying in a rack. It smelled like garlic, rosemary, and something bubbling gently in a cast iron pot.

Tom fired up the grill in the small backyard, and Dan stood beside him, a beer in hand, watching the coals settle. The light had softened, filtering through the lattice of still-bare branches overhead. Kira and Allison were inside prepping the salad, plates, and a warm flatbread that smelled faintly of cumin.

"Appreciate the help," Tom said, laying the steaks across the grates with a quiet sizzle. "I never get the timing right on these without someone watching."

"You mean without someone doing it for you," Dan said.

Tom grinned. "Exactly."

The grill hissed as a bit of fat hit the flame. They stood in companionable silence for a few minutes, the rhythm of gentle sizzling filling the space.

"I meant to say earlier," Tom added, "you handled that bear situation well. I know Ken wasn't thrilled, but I heard he signed off."

"He didn't have much choice," Dan said. "The bear was already sedated and loaded by the time I got him on the line."

Tom nodded. "Sometimes you've gotta make the call."

Dan didn't answer, but the corner of his mouth ticked upward slightly.

Inside, Kira opened the screen door and leaned out. "Veggie plate's almost ready. How are we looking?"

"Two minutes," Tom called back.

"Perfect," she said, then to Allison, "grab the glasses?"

They ate out back, close together, seated around a weathered picnic table Tom had salvaged from a trailhead project years ago. The steaks were thick and well-seared. Kira's veggie plate was bright with color, roasted carrots, charred cauliflower, fennel with lemon zest, and slid in front of Allison without comment, just a small smile.

Conversation meandered lightly—trail gossip, park politics, the latest broken boiler in the sheriff's office.

Allison spoke up now and then, mostly when Kira steered things toward gear or work. She seemed more at ease out here than she had by the river. The food helped, and so did the wine.

"Is this local?" she asked, holding her glass up.

"Palisade," Kira said. "Tom says it tastes like gravel, but I think it's decent."

"I said *earthy*," Tom muttered.

"You said *dirty*."

Another round of quiet laughter.

Dan leaned back, fork paused over a bite of steak, watching shadows stretch across the edge of the lawn.

After the plates were cleared and the sky had gone full dark, they moved inside. The living room was softly lit, just one floor lamp by the bookshelf and the faint blue from a speaker tucked in the corner, low music threading through the room.

Tom poured another round of wine. Kira curled into the arm of the couch with her knees up, barefoot now, her glass balanced easily in one hand.

Dan sat low in a wide chair across from her, legs stretched out. Allison perched beside him on the ottoman, flipping absently through a local magazine she'd picked up off the coffee table.

For a while, no one said much.

Then Kira broke the silence, her voice casual but thoughtful. "Do you ever think animals are more aware than we give them credit for?"

Tom gave a soft snort from the kitchen. "Aware of what?"

"Of each other. Of *us*. Of things we can't even measure."

Tom reentered the room with a handful of dark chocolate squares and passed them around. "They're smart. No doubt. But there's a line between instinct and consciousness. They don't think like we do."

"I'm not saying they think like we do," Kira said. "I'm saying maybe there's more to life than thinking."

Dan watched her over the rim of his glass. The flicker of interest in her tone wasn't new—but it touched a nerve, reaching something that lay just below the surface.

"You've seen the studies," she continued. "Elephants mourning their dead. Crows remembering faces. Octopuses solving puzzles and opening jars. We write it off as cleverness or mimicry, but... maybe we just don't have the language for it."

Tom sat down beside her. "I've also seen a fox chase its tail for twenty minutes straight. Doesn't mean it's on the brink of enlightenment."

Kira smiled. "Maybe it was just having a good time."

Allison let the magazine drop into her lap. "I don't know. I feel like we're always looking for ourselves in animals. Like we need them to be like us to matter."

"Maybe they matter in a different way," Dan murmured softly.

They all turned toward him.

He didn't elaborate.

Kira tilted her head slightly. "Exactly."

Tom shrugged. "I get it. But there's a reason we're at the top of the chain. Tools, language, consciousness. We're the only ones who've ever looked up and wondered why."

Kira leaned back, wine glass resting on her thigh. "Or maybe we're just the loudest."

A long moment passed. Outside, something rustled in the bushes—a raccoon or maybe just the wind.

Dan didn't say anything else. But something in him understood. Not thought. Not even a memory.

The wine stretched into comfort. Talk turned back around to favorite trail mishaps, weird wildlife calls, a time Tom accidentally locked his cruiser with the engine running and the radio blaring Johnny Cash.

It was easy.

Eventually, Kira looked over at Dan and Allison. "We've been meaning to get up to Leadville this spring.

Do the Healy House tour before the summer rush hits. Have you two ever been?"

Allison shook her head. "I've heard of it."

"It's great," Tom said. "Weird history. Ghost stories. And there's a cafe across the street that makes an ungodly good cinnamon roll."

Dan smiled. "We're in. Let us know when."

Kira raised her glass slightly. "It's a plan."

No one rushed to leave, and when they finally stood to go, the goodbyes were easy, unforced—see you soon, safe drive, let's not wait too long.

Outside, the air had cooled. Somewhere far off, a coyote yipped once, then fell silent.

Dan glanced back at the warmly lit doorway before climbing into the truck. The owl carving watched from its post, weathered and wise.

SIX

THE HEAT LINGERED even as the sun dipped behind the western ridge, casting long shadows across the narrow road that wound up into Redcliff. Dan turned off the engine, let the dust settle, and sat for a moment. Shankley shifted in the passenger seat.

"Yeah," Dan said contentedly, giving the dog's shoulder a pat. "Home."

He stepped out, stretched, and glanced up at the house. The porch light was on. Through the open window, he heard laughter, bright, quick, with a rhythm that didn't belong between him and Allison. It was a piece of her past, come to life in the present.

A second pair of boots sat by the door, scuffed leather with a chalky smear across one toe. A small climbing pack leaned against the wall—professional gear, expensive and well-used.

Inside, the kitchen was warm with the scent of slow roasted garlic. Allison stood at the stove, flipping something in a pan. At the kitchen table a woman sat, hair pulled back with a bent carabiner. Her faded tank top, cargo shorts, and relaxed confidence spoke of moving through the world on your own terms.

"You're back," Allison said, glancing over her shoulder. "This is Mara."

Dan had heard plenty about her. The epic hikes, the early starts, the three-day summit push that ended in a storm. Allison had told those stories with a kind of reverence, sometimes wistful, sometimes with a spark Dan couldn't quite name.

"Mara," Dan said, offering his hand. "Nice to finally meet you."

She stood to shake it. "You too. Ali's talked all about you. And this place, it's even better than I pictured."

Allison smiled. "She's headed to Rifle for a climb. Stopped in on the way."

"Figured I'd cash in on some home cooking and good company," Mara said, grinning. "Ali's the only one from college who didn't just *talk* about getting out west."

They sat down to eat—something light and lemony, with roasted vegetables and quinoa. Dan picked at it while Mara and Allison talked and laughed. Their conversation moved fast and easy, all shorthand and shared memories about lightning storms above the treeline. The time they ran out of daylight and had to bivy beneath a boulder, whispering bad jokes until morning.

Dan had heard most of it before, in pieces. But now, hearing Mara's voice wrap around those memories, it felt different, more vivid. Like he'd only ever known the outlines.

"We were thinking about hiking up to the ridgeline in the morning," Mara said, refilling her glass. "Maybe head up Notch Mountain a ways if the weather holds."

Allison looked over. "Is that okay?"

Dan nodded. "Of course. I'm heading out to McCoy tomorrow, but take the Tacoma, it could use a run out."

He stood, collecting a few empty plates. "I think I'll take Shankley for a walk. Let you two catch up properly."

Allison looked up and gave a quick smile. "We'll try not to burn the place down."

Dan had just reached for the leash when he caught Mara's voice behind him—easy, offhand: "Oh, and Boulder Backcountry's looking for a new assistant manager. It's a great gig, especially with your background. You'd be a natural."

Allison made a soft sound of interest, nothing more. But Dan had already turned, hand reaching for the door handle.

Dan clipped the leash to Shankley's collar and stepped out into the evening. The air had cooled, but the warmth of the day still clung to the pavement. A faint breeze came off the hillside, carrying the scent of pine, dry dust, and someone's backyard grill.

They turned right at the end of the drive, heading down Redcliff's main road, if it could be called that. Just a stretch of cracked asphalt, one block long, lined with sagging porches and secondhand mountain bikes leaning against rails.

Shankley nosed along the edge of the road, tail up, alert to the hidden dramas of weeds and fenceposts. Dan let the dog set the page.

He passed old man Carver sitting on his front steps, beer in hand, a battered Rockies cap pulled low.

"Evenin', Dan."

"Evenin', Carver."

Two houses down, a couple of kids were chalking dragons on the sidewalk. One of them waved, blue streaks on her fingers. Dan raised a hand in return.

Farther along, Mangos, Redcliff's bar, was alive with sound and light. Someone was playing guitar inside—live, or maybe just damn good speakers—and the warm, syncopated thump of bass spilled onto the street. Through the windows he caught flashes of raised glasses, elbows on tables, and snatches of conversations.

He paused across the street—watched it all without stepping in, then kept walking.

There was no unease in him. Just a quiet stillness, like the town itself had softened around the edges. He liked this part of evening, the in-between, when the world hadn't quite gone dark, and the outlines of things still held their shape.

Back at the house, laughter filtered through the open window again. Mara's voice, animated and full of motion. Allison replying, her laugh clearer now, more whole.

Dan smiled faintly. It was good to see her energized. Lit up like that. Lately she'd been quieter, tight around the eyes, like something inside was trying to rearrange itself and couldn't quite get there.

He didn't mind stepping back tonight.

Some stories didn't need him in them.

He gave Shankley a rub behind the ear and turned them toward the trailhead, letting the dog lead again. The stars were just starting to show above the ridge, faint and watchful.

By the time Dan circled back toward the house, the lights in the kitchen were glowing warm against the night. Shankley climbed up the steps ahead of him, tail wagging, before settling by the door.

Inside, Mara and Allison were still at the table, the remains of dinner pushed aside. Their voices rolled gently through the space—half-laughed stories, quick interjections, the kind of conversation that flowed without needing to be steered.

Dan paused in the doorway just long enough to smile.

"I'm gonna turn in," he said, not trying to interrupt. "Meeting with the sheep herders tomorrow. I should probably get my thoughts together for the talk."

Allison glanced over, eyes soft. "Right. Good luck with it."

Mara gave a small wave. "Nice meeting you properly."

"You too," Dan said, already walking down the hall. "Night."

He clicked off the hallway light, stepped into the bedroom, and sat on the edge of the bed to pull off his boots. Shankley had followed and sat down beside him with a sigh.

Dan rubbed his hands over his face. Tomorrow would come early.

SEVEN

The Colorado Parks and Wildlife field office in Eagle sat unobtrusively behind a chain-link fence, a squat tan building that held the lingering smell of damp clothes and burned coffee. Dan pushed through the side door and made his way down the narrow hallway toward the back office.

Ken was already at his desk, hunched over a tangle of printouts and trail camera stills. The office was small and spare, metal filing cabinets with dented corners, old topo maps curling at the edges, a coffee ring or two on the workbench, but everything had its place. The gear might've been ten years past new, but it all still worked. Just like the people using it. "You're early," Ken said without looking up.

Dan dropped his field bag by the door. "So are you."

"Not by choice. The printer's jammed again, and I'm trying to pull a clean copy of the McCoy grazing map before the meeting."

"Still using the same busted feed tray?"

Ken gave him a look. "The tray's not broken. You just have to know how to feed it."

Dan stepped over, thumped the side of the machine with practiced indifference, and gave the paper stack a gentle shuffle. It kicked into life with a shudder.

Ken grunted. "You should've gone into IT."

Dan shrugged. "Too frustrating."

Ken leaned back and rubbed his neck. "Alright, McCoy this morning. There's a sheep outfit about to head up for the season. They want reassurance. You'll be talking predators—wolves, obviously, but don't let them forget the usual suspects."

Dan nodded. "Coyotes, bears, lions."

"They're riled up because of what happened last summer over in Delta. There were a couple confirmed wolf kills. One guy claims he lost ten lambs, but we never got clean confirmation."

"I read the report," Dan said. "Predator tracks, but no scat. No visual ID."

Ken tapped the corner of a clipboard. "Exactly. Keep it calm. Remind them about the compensation protocols, but don't sugarcoat the restrictions. And..." He paused, then gestured toward the door. "You're not going alone."

Dan raised an eyebrow.

Ken stood. "Come on. He's out back checking the truck, you can take that today."

They stepped outside into the bright morning. The air was still cool, carrying that faint bite of sagebrush and irrigation runoff. A white state truck was backed into the lot, and behind it knelt a lanky guy with short, sun-bleached hair, fiddling with a torque wrench.

"Sean!" Ken barked. "You break it, you're walking."

The kid stood and wiped his hands on his cargo pants. "Just tightening the hitch—it wasn't sitting right."

Ken turned to Dan. "Dan, meet Sean Lauder. He transferred up from Alamosa. Only a couple of months in with CPW. He's going to ride with you today."

Sean stepped forward and offered a hand. "Heard a lot about you, man. You're the guy who tranquilized that bear in a dumpster, one handed, right?"

Dan gave the hand a firm shake. "That's a bit of a stretch. But yeah. That was me."

"Cool," Sean said, clearly trying not to seem too eager. "I'm looking forward to learning from you."

Dan glanced at Ken, who gave him the faintest smirk.

"The truck's gassed up," Ken said. "Maps are on the dash. And don't forget the Spanish handouts."

Dan opened the passenger door and peeked inside. Neatly stacked papers. Fresh copies. Bottled water. Sean had done his homework.

"Alright," Dan said, tossing his bag into the cab. "Let's see how McCoy's feeling this spring."

The drive passed easily, early summer sun slanting over the hills, the road warm and familiar beneath the tires. No wind. No weather. Just the slow climb north through open country. The cottonwoods along the river had filled out since Dan was last this way, their leaves popping green with spring growth.

Sean sat in the passenger seat, sipping from a plastic travel mug, his boots still dusty from some trail or other.

"So," he said, "how do you tell a lion track from a big dog, if it's not super clear?"

Dan glanced at him, then back at the road. "Check the symmetry. Dog prints usually line up—lion's got a longer middle toe and the pad's more uneven. No claw marks, usually."

Sean nodded, chewing on that. "We had a lion kill a deer close to home once. This was before I was with CDW. Never saw the cat, I was hiking and found a kill site, a young deer, half-covered with leaves and grass. Pretty wild."

Dan nodded. "Classic lion behavior. They stash what they don't finish."

Dan glanced over. "Are you from Alamosa, or just worked there?"

"Yeah, I grew up there," Sean said. "Always love seeing the Sangres out the window every morning."

"Have you been up this way before?" Dan asked.

Sean shook his head. "First time. Looks... dry."

"Mostly mule deer through here," Dan said. "They browse on bitterbrush and sage this time of year. There's coyotes, the odd lion, sometimes a black bear up high."

Dan glanced at him. "D'you know how to tell if deer have been pushed by predators?"

Sean hesitated. "Scattered tracks, maybe? Or... I don't know... if they're running blind?"

Dan gave a small nod. "Not bad. Watch their grouping. If they're bunched tight, heads up, moving erratic—it usually means something's been nosing around. Calm herds spread out more, graze slower. It's subtle, but you'll learn to read it."

As they pulled in, the road narrowed to a wide gravel loop ringed by a handful of parked pickups and faded trailers. Four shepherd caravans sat off to one side—stubby, sun-bleached wagons on weathered wheels, their roofs strapped down with blue tarps and firewood stacked neatly beside them. A battered stock trailer was backed up near one, and a pen held a cluster of horses and dogs, tethered in the shade.

Dan slowed to a stop and let the engine idle. "This is base. They tow those out early in the season—up near the grazing allotments. Each herder gets a caravan, a few dogs, and a radio. Most of them won't come back until the end of the summer."

Sean leaned forward, taking in the scene. "They live up there all summer?"

"Yeah," Dan said. "It's solitary work. They move with the herd, try to keep them off private land and away from the predators. Not always easy."

He shut off the truck and the silence settled thick—just a stirring of wind and a faint creak from one of the caravans.

"C'mon," Dan said, reaching for the door. "Let's go meet 'em."

As Dan and Sean stepped out of the truck, a man emerged from behind one of the caravans, wiping his hands on a faded cloth. He wore a brimmed canvas hat and a vest over a long-sleeve shirt despite the heat. His weathered face broke into a brief smile.

"Morning, Dan."

"Luis." Dan shook his hand. "Appreciate you gathering the crew."

Luis nodded, then looked toward Sean.

"This is Sean Lauder," Dan said. "New to our district and learning the ropes."

"Welcome." Luis gave Sean a solid handshake. "Been a while since CPW sent two at once."

"Thought I'd give him the full tour," Dan said.

A few yards away, four herders leaned in the shade of the caravans. Their faces were sun-darkened, eyes wary but attentive. One smoked, the others watched quietly. Dan raised a hand.

"Buenos días."

They responded in kind—one with a nod, another with a quiet "buen día."

Luis turned slightly. "These are the boys running the sheep this season. Jairo, César, Miguel, and the tall one's Óscar. They'll be heading up to the range in a few days."

Dan nodded. "Glad to meet you."

He looked back to Luis. "We're here to go over predator activity—recent sightings, signs to watch for, what to report, what not to worry about. Ken said you've had some concerns come up already."

Luis gave a slight shrug. "Some prints by the high pasture last week. Maybe lion, maybe not. One of the dogs barked hard at something just after dusk. Hard to say."

He hesitated a moment, then added, "There's talk about wolves, too. Ones they released. Heard a few might've come this far north."

Dan nodded. "You're not the only one asking. I'll cover that."

They gathered in the shade behind the caravans, the late-morning heat already creeping up off the gravel. One of the herders rolled a stump over to sit on; another leaned back against the side of a trailer, arms crossed. Luis stood off to the side, his brow already creased with a question.

Dan took a breath, glanced around, and began.

"Thanks for making time," he said. "I know the season's just getting started, but it's good to stay ahead of things. You'll be moving out soon, and we want everyone on the same page about predators—what's common, what's not, and how to handle it if something shows up."

Luis translated as he went, pausing between sentences to speak clearly and evenly in Spanish. The herders nodded along, quiet and attentive.

"Coyotes are still the most common predator in this area," Dan continued. "You'll hear them at night, sometimes see tracks. They'll test the edges of a herd, especially if the dogs are distracted. Keep the dogs close and fed, don't leave scraps out, and move your bedding ground every few nights if you're in a tight spot."

He shifted slightly, meeting Luis's eye for the next part.

"As for lions, we've had a few sightings down near Yarmony Ridge, but nothing recent this far north. They're solitary, move at night, and usually avoid large groups. If one does show, they tend to go after smaller or injured sheep. The same rules apply, keep the herd tight, dogs alert, and let us know if you see signs."

Luis gave a short nod and passed it along.

Dan paused before continuing, letting the moment settle.

"Now, about the wolves."

The herders stirred slightly, eyes narrowing, the word familiar enough.

"I know there's been talk," Dan said, "and yes, wolves were reintroduced in Colorado. Mostly to the north and west of here. So far, we don't have confirmed tracks in this area, but it's possible they'll range further over time."

He kept his tone calm, steady.

"They're smart, cautious, and travel far. But they're not common here. If they show up, you'll probably hear them before you see them. Howling at night, or coordinated movement near the herd."

Luis translated carefully, glancing at Dan mid-sentence to make sure he had it right.

"Now, if a sheep is taken by a predator," Dan went on, "you need to report it. Take photos. Note the location. The state has a compensation program in place. If we can verify a loss, there's money to cover it, but you have to document it, especially with wolves."

He looked directly at Luis now.

"And wolves are protected. No shooting. No trapping. If you see one near the herd, call it in. Immediately. We'll respond. But no independent action unless there's a clear threat to human life. That's the law."

Luis nodded slowly, translating with a slight tightening around the mouth. The herders looked more serious now, but none spoke.

Dan softened slightly. "We don't expect problems. Most of the time, it's coyotes. Sometimes a stray dog. Just stay alert, keep the herd moving, and work with the dogs. You know the land. Trust your instincts."

He stepped back slightly. "That's it from me. Questions?"

Luis asked in Spanish, but the herders only shook their heads or murmured "no."

Dan nodded once. "All right. You're good men doing hard work. We'll stay in touch."

He turned to Sean. "Grab the water bottles from the truck, and the handouts. We'll leave a set with Luis."

Sean gave a quick nod and moved toward the truck, glad to have something concrete to do.

As the herders drifted back to their caravans, Luis stepped beside Dan and motioned toward the ridgeline. "Jairo saw something up past the first rise yesterday. Tracks, maybe scat. You've got time?"

Dan glanced at Sean, then back at Luis. "Sure. Let's take a look."

Jairo was already tightening the laces on his boots. He said little, just gave Dan a nod and set off with a quiet, measured gait. Dan and Sean followed, the ground sloping gently upward into dry brush and scattered pines.

It was cooler in the trees, the air holding a faint smell of sage. They moved carefully, Jairo pointing now and then to broken earth or faint depressions in the grass. Sean stayed close behind, scanning the ground and taking it in.

A few hundred yards up, near a stand of young juniper, Jairo paused and pointed at a patch of disturbed soil beneath a fallen branch.

Dan crouched low. "Coyote," he said, after a moment. "It's an older track, maybe two days."

Jairo nodded and moved a few steps off to the side, eyes down.

Sean leaned in. "What gives it away?"

Dan traced a shape in the dirt with one finger. "Narrow toe spread. Claw marks. See how the pads are almost in line? Coyotes move clean when they're trotting."

Sean nodded, absorbing it.

They walked a little farther. Dan scanned instinctively, eyes flicking to the base of brush, to shaded patches of ground, to what the land wanted to give away.

Then he stopped.

Near a stand of rabbitbrush, of course, was a small cluster of pellets, dry and pinched at one end, scattered loosely in the dust.

Dan knelt. Picked one up between thumb and forefinger.

"Rabbit," he said softly. "Not fresh, but recent."

He held the pellet a moment longer than he needed to. It was light and dry, but there was something in the smell—subtle, earthy, like rain on dust—that hit a note he hadn't been expecting. He exhaled slowly and set it down.

Sean crouched beside him. "Are they a sign of predators?"

Dan shook his head. "Just rabbits being rabbits."

But he didn't move right away. There was something quiet in the air here. A stillness. A tension that wasn't a threat but wasn't entirely calm either.

He stood, brushed his hands, and nodded toward Jairo. "Let's circle back."

By the time they made it back to the base, the sun had climbed higher, baking the gravel and casting sharp shadows beneath the caravans. The herders were gathered in a loose circle, drinking water and checking gear. One was stretched out in the shade, hat pulled low over his face.

Jairo peeled off without a word, heading for his trailer.

Luis met them near the truck. "Find anything?"

Dan nodded. "Old coyote sign. Nothing fresh. There are plenty of rabbits up there too."

Luis gave a short grunt, somewhere between acknowledgement and amusement. "They'll eat better than we do."

Dan opened the driver's door. "Luis, you've got my number? I'll check back through later in the season."

Luis nodded. "Appreciate it. Not everyone makes time to come up here."

Dan met his eye. "Our job's to make things work, for everyone. We'll keep checking in."

Sean handed out the last of the water bottles, and Dan paused for a moment, letting the dry air settle.

Then he climbed in, gave a final wave, and turned the key. The truck rumbled to life. Dust kicked up behind them as they rolled out, the caravans shrinking in the rearview mirror—small, sun-bleached islands in a sea of sage and stone.

As they bumped back onto the gravel road, the truck picked up speed. For a while, neither of them spoke.

Then Dan said, mostly to the windshield, "That's the part of the job nobody writes down, just showing up."

They'd been driving for about twenty minutes when Dan slowed, then eased the truck off the road onto a flat stretch of hardpan. No sign, no fence gate, just a break in the sage and a narrow rise that looked out over a wide drainage to the west.

Sean looked over. "Something up?"

Dan shook his head. "Just a minute."

He stepped out into the heat. The wind had died down, and the air held a dry, metallic edge. The land felt still, too still, maybe. He walked a few paces beyond the truck and crouched near a tangle of low brush, resting his hand on the ground.

The soil crumbled under his fingers, dry on top, cool just below. It held the scent of dust and heat, but something else too. Something he'd carried with him since that moment on the slope above the herders' camp.

Rabbit.

It came back sharper than he expected. The small, dry pellet. The way he'd held it a moment too long. The smell was earthy, almost sharp.

He closed his eyes.

Behind him, the engine ticked as it cooled. Sean's door creaked open, then shut again with a hollow clunk.

"Find something?" Sean asked softly.

Dan didn't answer right away.

There was a sound in the grass to his left, small and sudden. A flicker of motion. Too fast to see clearly. Not threatening. Just alive.

He turned his head slowly and listened. There was no wind. No birdsong. Just the faint hum of heat rising off the land.

His breath caught. A feeling, unexpected. A narrowing. A shift.

Stillness.

Something in him leaned toward it.

He stayed crouched, one hand pressed to the soil, the other resting on his knee. The muscles in his legs felt tight and spring-loaded. A current ran through them, low and electric, like a held breath with nowhere to go.

The smell of the dirt deepened. That dry, sun-cracked smell layered with roots, fur, and the faint ammonia trace of scat. It wasn't unpleasant. It was honest. Familiar in a way that had no language.

He blinked.

The world was brighter. The colors raw. Shadows deeper.

His heartbeat slowed, then quickened, fast and light. Thump-thump-thump. Not fear. Alertness. Every muscle drawn taut, every nerve alive to the tilt of the earth.

Somewhere in the grass behind him, there was movement, a hawk overhead, maybe. Or the idea of one.

He turned his head too fast. The bones in his neck felt wrong. His ears burned, then receded, then shifted entirely, like they weren't where they used to be.

His field of vision widened and flattened. The depth was strange, but the motion was perfect. A leaf flicked in the brush, and he saw it all. Every stutter of air, every tremble of grass.

Dan wasn't gone—just... distant. Watching.

The body knew what to do.

Stillness. Wait. Listen.

The next moment, there was motion. Sudden, clean, and low to the ground.

Through brush. Through earth. The scrape of paws, made for speed, made for escape.

The world became immediate. Not thought but instinct. Cover. Shadow. The cool belly of a burrow somewhere ahead. Every sound mattered. Every vibration carried meaning.

There was no fear. Only the truth of being prey.

The rabbit moved like water under tension—low and quick, always listening. Muscles coiled and released with purpose, no waste, no noise.

It slipped through sage, past a rock worn smooth by wind, through a patch of grass no taller than a boot and paused with its nose twitching and ears high. The world was built of scent and vibration—noises trembled through the ground like warnings passed hand to mouth.

The hawk was gone, but the memory of it lingered. A shadow that lived in the blood.

There were predators, yes. Sharp and visible. The fox. The eagle. The snap of a trap.

But there were other dangers, too. Older. Less direct.

The rabbit stilled again. Remembering. A trace in the marrow. Something passed down.

Sickness.

Not now. Not here. But in the memory of the body. In the scent of a burrow long abandoned. In the hesitation before a grooming paw met a mate's fur. Inside the blood like a waiting ember.

There had been a time, not long ago, when sickness came. Something in the flesh that turned good bodies bad. Eyes swollen. Skin broken. Warrens stilled by dawn.

The rabbit didn't name it; rabbits had no words. But it knew. Knew that not all death came with teeth, beak, or claw.

The rabbit was healthy. Quick. Strong.

But it was not immune.

It never forgot.

And neither, somewhere deep inside, did Dan.

The sound came first—not a predator's rustle or the tremor of the earth, but something thinner. Higher. A human shape.

"...Dan?"

It floated above the instinct, tugging at the thread of who he was.

"You okay?"

A pause.

"You seemed a bit out of it."

Dan blinked.

The world flattened and colors dulled. His legs were cramped from crouching, knees stiff. One hand was still pressed to the dirt, warm now from the sun, dry and real beneath his palm.

Sean stood a few feet away, brow creased, one hand on his hip. Watching.

Dan straightened carefully, brushing dust from his hand. "Yeah," he said, his voice low. "I'm good."

He didn't look back at the brush.

The moment had passed. But it hadn't gone.

It lived in his bones now. In the knowledge of softness. Of speed. Of vulnerability without shame. Of sickness that passed easily between bodies.

Dan walked back to the truck without another word.

Eight

Ken handed over a printed report without looking up from his screen. "I'd like you to check Pitkin tomorrow," he said. "There's been a couple of reported sightings, mountain goats near the lake. If they're lingering, I'd like confirmation."

Dan scanned the map clipped to the front. "Do you want photos?"

"If you can get 'em. But mainly just eyes on the animals. That trail's no joke, so I recommend going early."

Out in the lot behind the CPW field office, Dan was unfolding a map when Sean wandered up, still in his field gear.

"You're really hiking Pitkin with the dog?" Sean asked, leaning against the truck, arms folded.

"Yeah," Dan said, glancing at the topo map spread across the hood. "CPW's had a few sightings logged, a couple of mountain goats near the lake. Ken figured it's worth getting a look at them."

Sean gave a low whistle. "That's a haul for a maybe."

Dan shrugged. "Good excuse to get up high. Allison's coming too."

"She's the one that climbs, right?"

"Strong hiker," Dan said. "She's been up there before."

Sean looked down at Shankley, who was nosing around the gravel lot behind the CPW office. "And you're hauling this guy along?"

"That's the plan. But it's wilderness the whole way—he'd have to be leashed from the trailhead."

"Ten miles on a short rope? That's not a good day for a dog."

Dan sighed. "No, it's not."

Sean rubbed the back of his neck, thinking. "Tell you what. I've got deer fence checks tomorrow. He can ride along with me if you like?"

Dan looked at him. "You sure?"

"Yeah. It's easy duty. He'll get more out of it than hiking tethered to your hip."

Dan hesitated, then nodded. "How are you settling in?" he asked. "It feels like you've been here a while now."

"Three weeks Monday," Sean said. "Guess that makes me almost a local."

Dan smiled. "Long enough to get assigned fence duty, anyway."

"What can I say, rookie assignment, but the fences need checking."

Dan glanced at Shankley, who was now curled at the base of the office steps, ears flicking at the early evening sounds. "Alright. He's yours for the day."

"I'll take him today if that works, save the early pickup." Sean said, giving the leash a tug. "You'll be wheels-up by what, six?"

"Closer to five," Dan said. "I told Allison we need to be on the trail before the sun hits."

Sean shook his head, smiling. "Better you than me, man."

Dan watched them head off, Sean whistling, Shankley trotting beside him, then turned back toward the truck.

* * *

The trail climbed steeply right from the start, with tight switchbacks carved into hard-packed dirt, root-knotted and shaded by dense lodgepole pine. Dan leaned into the slope, lungs working, his boots finding a rhythm on the uneven grade. Behind him, Allison kept pace, her breathing steady but audible. Neither of them spoke. Not out of tension, just focus. The quiet that came when effort demanded attention.

It was a proper haul. The type of hike that settled into your legs and stayed there, that rewarded you slowly.

The first landmark was the waterfall. They heard it well before they saw it—a low roar rising through the trees like a breath from the mountain itself. The trail curled alongside it briefly, close enough to feel the mist spitting out from where meltwater dropped fast over dark rock, emptying into a pool below. Dan paused to let the cool air hit his face, chest rising, damp shirt clinging to his back.

"Strong this year," he said, though mostly to himself.

Allison gave a short nod, hands on her hips, and kept moving. He followed.

The climb didn't let up. Even when it eased, it never truly let go. The forest thinned, then thickened again—first lodgepole, then stands of aspen with their pale trunks and whispering leaves. The sound of water faded behind them, replaced by the hush of breeze and bootfall. Dan wiped his forearm across his brow. His shirt was soaked. There was satisfaction in it.

Then came the wildflowers. They burst along the edges of the trail and into the clearings—bright brushstrokes of color against the green. Scarlet paintbrush, clusters of lupines, the sharp yellow of balsamroot. Dan slowed a little as the incline softened, taking them in.

"That one's lupinus argenteus," he said, pointing. "Lupine."

Allison raised a brow. "Getting fancy?"

"Only one I remember in Latin."

"What about that red one?"

"Indian paintbrush."

"No Latin?"

He grinned. "Just paintbrush."

They kept moving. Legs burning now, in that good way, like their bodies had found the groove. Higher up, the trail opened briefly along the shoulder of the ridge, and the Gore Range made its entrance with sharp peaks lined up like broken stone teeth, snow lingering in shaded cuts. They didn't say anything, but walked a little slower.

The air changed as they climbed, thinner and cooler. The trees gave way to scrub, the sky widening above them.

And then the lake.

It arrived like a secret. Just a break in the trail, a few more steps, and there it was: still, clear, and pristine. The surface reflecting the sky, holding it without a ripple. Rocks lined the shore, bleached smooth by snowmelt and time.

Dan let his pack slide to the ground, chest rising hard, sweat drying on his back. "We're first," he said, his voice low.

Allison stepped beside him, pulling off her sunglasses. Her breath was still catching up to her body, but she didn't speak. She just looked.

The effort sat with them, quietly earned. In the legs. In the lungs. In the silence of arrival.

The peaks watched from above. The water kept still.

And for a while, they did too.

They found a flat patch near the water, where a few sun-warmed boulders sat clustered like ancient furniture. Dan shrugged off his pack and unzipped the top pocket, pulling out a pair of sandwiches wrapped in wax paper and a small container of trail mix.

Allison dropped onto one of the rocks, stretching out her legs with a groan. "That was no walk in the park."

Dan passed her a sandwich and sat nearby. "You're not wrong."

They ate in companionable silence for a while. The lake lay still before them, framed by rock and sky. Every so often, a breeze moved through the high grasses at the shore's edge, sending ripples across the surface like breath.

A patch of white caught the eye, high above the far slope.

Three goats had appeared near the scree field above the eastern rim, white against the darker rock, slow-moving and surefooted. One adult, two younger. They stepped with calm precision, winding across the ledge as if the drop below didn't exist.

Dan lowered the last of his sandwich and watched them.

"They're often here," he murmured.

Allison followed his gaze. "Must be a decent mineral lick somewhere."

He nodded absently, eyes on the largest goat. It had stopped to glance down toward them, head lifting, ears forward. Not alarmed. Just—noticing.

Dan tilted his head slightly, squinting into the bright.

He wondered, not for the first time, what it meant to see the world from that vantage. To live that high and that sure. What did the terrain look like from hooves and instinct? Did they mark time? Did they feel awe? Or just wind and stone and the drive of their own hunger?

The goat moved again. The younger ones followed, light-footed across the slope.

Dan let out a slow breath. "I wonder what they think of us."

Allison glanced over. "Probably that we're loud. And sweaty."

Dan smiled faintly. "Fair enough."

He popped a few almonds into his mouth and leaned back on his elbows, gaze drifting across the lake. The sunlight had shifted, brushing the far shore with gold. Somewhere behind them, a bird called out, sharp and quick.

For a little while, they said nothing. Just sat with tired legs and open sky.

The quiet didn't last.

Voices carried up the trail, echoing in the thin mountain air. A group was nearing the lake, maybe four or five people. Dan could hear the scrape of hiking poles, the uneven rhythm of footsteps on rock. Then the yip of a dog, high and eager.

He sat up straighter.

Allison turned too. "Please tell me that dog's leashed."

It wasn't.

A blur of motion broke from the trail: a lean, tan dog, some kind of shepherd mix, ears forward, tongue lolling, barreling straight for the ridgeline where the goats still lingered. It let out a high, excited bark and took off at a full run toward the slope.

The goats scattered.

The big one wheeled uphill with a startled jump. The two younger ones darted after, fast and jittery, hooves scrabbling against the rock as they disappeared into the high basin beyond view.

"Goddammit," Dan muttered, already on his feet.

The group emerged seconds later—two men, two women, a teenage boy, all kitted out in bright technical gear. One of the women shaded her eyes, watching the dog with a laugh. "He's just stretching his legs," she called to no one in particular.

Dan stepped forward. "That's a violation."

They all looked at him now, blinking like they hadn't quite registered he was there.

The man in front with a gray goatee and mirrored sunglasses, gave a nonchalant shrug. "Relax, it's public land."

Dan kept his voice steady. "You're in designated wilderness. Off-leash dogs harassing wildlife is illegal. Especially goats—they're protected in this zone."

The woman tried to call the dog back, but it was already out of earshot, bounding uphill through the rocks like it owned the range.

The man scoffed. "Come on. It's just a couple of goats. They're fine."

Dan stepped closer. "I'm with Colorado Parks and Wildlife."

That got their attention.

Dan pulled out his badge wallet and flipped it open. "You'll need to leash your dog. Now. And I'm issuing a citation."

"Are you serious?" the man said. "He's a good dog."

Dan didn't blink. "I'm sure he is. This isn't about the dog, it's about you. It's your responsibility to keep him leashed. Especially in a place like this."

He gestured toward the ridgeline, where the goats had vanished. "This is a fragile alpine zone. Those goats are already under pressure from heat, predators, and dwindling range, and now, human disturbance. Your dog just triggered a full flight response. That kind of stress can cause injury. Separation from young. That's not on the dog. That's on you."

He scribbled the details on the citation pad, methodical.

The teenage boy sulked behind his sunglasses, muttering something. One of the women glared. The other finally caught the dog and clipped a leash to its collar, tugging it back toward the group with visible effort.

Dan handed the ticket over. "Violation of Title 33. Harassment of wildlife by domestic animals. It's not minor."

The man stared at it like it was written in another language. "We're just trying to enjoy the mountains."

"So were the goats," Dan said. Then he turned and walked away.

Back by the lake, Allison hadn't moved. She was watching the group, her expression unreadable.

They packed up quietly. No more food, no more idle talk. The peace from earlier, broken.

As they headed back down the trail, the lake behind them settled into stillness again—but it was a different stillness than before.

Not untouched.

Just... enduring.

Dan turned once more, eyes lifting toward the slope where the goats had stood. The high ledge was empty, just sunlight on stone and a faint drift of wind in the alpine grass.

He tried, for a moment, to imagine the world from their view. The constant alertness. The need to read the land with every step—sound, scent, shadow. No margin for error. Then a dog comes, not hunting, not hungry, just thoughtless and fast. And the body reacts—flight, instinct, a jolt of old panic.

It wasn't malice. But it didn't have to be.

Allison's voice broke the thought. "They'll be fine. Mountain goats aren't exactly delicate."

Dan didn't answer. Just gave a small nod and turned back to the trail.

The trail fell away beneath their feet, winding back through wind-tossed grasses and down into the stands of aspen and pine. Allison walked a little ahead, her stride steady and efficient. The air had warmed since morning, and bees hovered near wildflowers, their small industry unbothered by the passing of humans.

Dan let the silence stretch, then closed the distance slightly.

"They're so alert," he said. "The goats. Everything in them tuned to the land. Like... they feel everything. Every sound, every shadow—it matters."

Allison glanced over her shoulder but kept walking. "Sure," she said. "Survival makes you pay attention."

Dan hesitated. "Yeah, but it's more than that. It's not just fear. There's... a kind of knowing. I don't know how to explain it. I just sometimes feel like I can almost *sense* what they're feeling."

She slowed a little but didn't stop. "You mean empathy?"

"Maybe. I don't know. It's like being near them opens something up. Makes the human stuff feel... noisy."

Allison stepped over a root and adjusted the strap on her pack. "Maybe you just needed a quiet hike."

Dan gave a small, breathy laugh. "Maybe."

They walked on.

The trail wound deeper into the trees, light shifting through the canopy. Between their footsteps, only the hush of wind through pine.

Whatever else he might've said held back inside him.

As the trail eased into its final descent, the trees grew taller and denser, the light breaking in long, slanting shards through the canopy.

Allison adjusted her pack strap and slowed slightly, falling into step beside Dan.

"I meant to tell you," she said. "There's a role opening at Boulder Basecamp. Merchandise and purchasing manager."

Dan looked over, eyebrows raised slightly.

"It's a step up," she went on. "Not just displays and inventory, I'd be overseeing seasonal buys, vendor relationships, product analysis. Basically running the whole gear floor from the back end."

He nodded but didn't say anything.

She glanced at him, then back to the trail. "If I want to stay in the industry, I've got to move forward. I can't keep floating between assistant roles. This is the kind of position that leads to regional work, maybe brand-side down the line."

Dan's face didn't change. Just the steady rhythm of his boots on the trail.

"I'm going to check it out," she said more firmly. "Doesn't mean I'm leaving tomorrow. Just—there's only so many windows."

Dan gave a slow nod. "Yeah. I get it."

The parking lot shimmered ahead through the trees, flashes of sun off windshields. Voices carried. The smell of warm asphalt filtered in.

Whatever had lived at the lake—stillness, wildness, whatever Dan had felt with the goats—was already slipping behind them.

At the trailhead, Dan eased his pack off and set it down gently in the dust. The small parking area was almost full, a late arrival pulling in. Allison had already climbed into the driver's seat, stretching her legs out and scrolling absently through her phone. Her hair was damp with sweat; cheeks flushed from the descent.

He stood for a moment at the edge of the lot, facing back toward the forest. The ridgeline was out of sight now, hidden behind folds of pine and aspen. But he pictured the goats anyway—still high above, skittish and watchful. He imagined their ears still twitching at every echo of human movement. How it must feel to live like that. Always alert. Always outnumbered.

"Hey," Allison called through the open window. "Are you good?"

Dan turned slightly. "Yeah. Just... needed a second."

She nodded and took a sip from her bottle. "I'm going to text Mara about that Boulder position. She knows the hiring manager."

Dan didn't reply at all. He closed the tailgate softly and walked around to the passenger side. The door creaked as he opened it.

Inside, the cab was warm with the smell of trail dust and old pine needles.

As he buckled his seatbelt, Allison added, not quite looking at him, "I'm going to apply. It's the right move if I want to stay in this industry long-term. Merchandising and purchasing. Big picture stuff. I'd be part of the seasonal planning team."

Dan gave a small nod.

She watched him, then turned the key. The engine started with a low hum.

They pulled out onto the asphalt, a quiet space settling between them, neither heavy nor light. Just... there.

Behind them, the mountains held their shape, indifferent as ever.

NINE

TOM'S SUV ROLLED UP TO THE CURB in front of Dan and Allison's place in Redcliff. Tom waved as Dan emerged from the small house and lowered the window with a grin. "Figured we'd drive. All you mountain town folks only own trucks, plenty of room for you in the back seat."

Kira leaned over from the passenger seat. "Today's history lesson begins at the Healy House, to be continued at the Silver Dollar Saloon."

Allison climbed into the back, settling in with a smile.

Dan leaned back in his seat, catching sight of Allison, who looked more relaxed than he'd seen her in a while. He could feel the day stretching ahead—a brief respite, a chance to breathe.

They climbed up to Leadville, with the windows cracked, sun glare flashing off the river that ran close to the road. They passed Camp Hale, the Second World War training ground for winter warfare, then Tennessee Pass and Ski Cooper, before the terrain opened to high plains of Leadville, where fourteen-thousand-foot peaks of the Collegiate Range stretched into the distance.

As they made the final turn, the town unfurled in front of them—some new buildings going up, a patchwork of clapboard buildings, a gas station and a grocery store before they hit the heart of town. The main street in Leadville ran wide and straight, flanked by weathered brick buildings with tall false fronts and the lingering feel of a town with plenty to remember.

Tom slowed the SUV and nodded toward the hub of town. "Still standing," he said. "Mostly."

Kira leaned forward, eyes sweeping the view. "It's like it never made up its mind, halfway between a boomtown and a ghost town."

Dan smiled faintly but didn't reply. He was watching the buildings and how they sat heavy against the sky, their edges worn, softened by time.

They passed a row of angled parking spots, a brick church with a wooden bell tower, and an old saloon with a painted sign barely legible from the road.

Tom turned onto a side street and pulled into a spot near the corner. "Alright. History time."

Allison was already unbuckling. "I've never actually been inside the Healy House."

Kira smiled. "You're going to love it."

The door to the Healy House creaked softly as they stepped inside. The air was cool but tinged with a staleness that sometimes lingers in historic homes. A woman behind the front desk looked up from a clipboard, her reading glasses perched halfway down her nose.

"Morning," she said, voice warm but not over-eager. "You folks just visiting today?"

Tom nodded. "Thought we'd play tourist."

The woman smiled. "Ah locals—I could have guessed. Where from?"

"Redcliff," Dan offered. "And down valley. Eagle."

"Well, you didn't come far, but hopefully you're ready to dive back in time."

Kira grinned.

Allison smiled. "Where should we start?"

"You should start with the Dexter Cabin, next door, then come back into the house. It's self-guided, but I'm around if you have questions. Watch your step upstairs—floors creak and lean like a Leadville old-timer."

Allison glanced back as they moved away from the desk. "She seems like she belongs here."

Dan gave a faint nod. "Yeah. Some people find their place."

They stepped back outside, the morning light now slanting brighter across the lawn. Just to the right of the house stood a low log structure with a shingled roof and a hand-carved sign that read: Dexter Cabin – circa 1879.

Tom whistled softly. "Looks like a trapper's lodge."

Kira pushed the door open and peered inside. "More like a gentleman's getaway, apparently."

Inside, the cabin was tidy and dim, its log walls chinked tight, the floor slanted just enough to feel it. A heavy table stood in the center, surrounded by mismatched chairs. On it sat a display case holding old poker chips, a worn deck of cards, and a silver flask tarnished with age.

Allison leaned in to read the placard. "James Dexter. Banker, speculator, poker enthusiast. Hosted an exclusive club for Leadville's elite."

Tom chuckled. "Now there's a phrase."

Kira read over her shoulder. "'Members included railroad tycoons, mine owners, and visiting dignitaries. Gambling was common, but the real currency was information.'"

Dan glanced around the small room—the desk in the corner, a spittoon near the stove, the framed photo of a man with a waxed mustache and the confident stare of someone used to winning.

"Feels like a place where things were decided," he said.

Tom nodded. "Deals made behind closed doors. Then someone walked out richer—or ruined."

They stepped back into the light, the cabin behind them falling quiet once again, just as it had for more than a hundred years.

The friends entered the house again and Allison offered a smile to the woman at the desk. "That cabin is something else. You can almost hear the cards hitting the table."

The guide returned the smile. "It's a pity that the walls can't talk."

The stairs creaked under their weight as they climbed, narrow and slightly tilted. Upstairs, the hallway opened into a string of small rooms—simple beds, washstands, patterned wallpaper faded to softness.

Kira ran her fingers lightly along the banister. "I love places like this."

Tom stepped into one of the bedrooms and let out a low whistle. "Ceiling's about six inches too short for me."

Allison read a framed panel mounted beside the doorframe. "It says the house started as a private residence—built in 1878 by August Meyer. He brought his bride here from St. Louis."

Dan stepped beside her, eyes scanning the room. "Then it became a guesthouse?"

She nodded. "Off and on. Families, boarders, travelers. It kept shifting depending on the economy—mining booms, silver busts."

Kira joined them. "That's kind of perfect. Nothing here ever stays one thing for long."

The guide's words echoed faintly from downstairs: *'The floors lean like the stories they keep.'*

Dan looked toward the window, where morning light fell through lace curtains in soft squares. He imagined the cycles—the quiet and the noise, the waiting and the rush. A home, then a stopover, then maybe a home again.

"It held on," he said softly.

Allison glanced at him. "What?"

"This place. It changed, but it held on. People kept finding ways to make it work."

She studied him for a second but didn't push. Just said, "That's Leadville, I guess."

They moved into the next room. Along one wall, a series of framed black-and-white photographs hung in neat rows, moments frozen in the brittle silver of the past.

Kira was the first to speak. "Oh, wow," she said, stepping closer to a portrait near the center.

Allison joined her. "Is that...?"

"A post-mortem photo," Kira confirmed, tilting her head. "Look at the lace collar. That's a child."

The girl in the image was wearing a beautiful white dress, hands folded neatly across her lap, eyes closed. Flowers framed the shot. It could almost be peaceful, except for the stillness. The wrong kind.

"Families used to pose them like that," Allison said softly. "It was the only way to remember them."

They lingered there, voices low, drawn to the delicate intimacy of grief preserved.

But Dan didn't join them. He'd stopped a few steps earlier, facing a different photograph entirely—an overhead view of Leadville during its peak. Or what passed for it.

There were no trees in the frame. Just slag piles, scorched hillsides, raw roads cut straight through once-living ground. Palls of smoke hung over the scene, the mines gaped open like wounds.

He didn't speak. Just stared.

It reminded him of photographs from Hiroshima—the aftermath. The flattened vista. A city gone to ash. This wasn't that, not exactly. But it had the same absence. The same imprint of destruction—something powerful and careless, moving through and leaving ruin in its place.

Tom came up behind him. "Hell of a shot, huh? Look at it now, the trees grew back."

Dan didn't answer right away. His eyes were still on the raw, treeless slopes, the skeletal outlines of structures built for one thing: extraction.

"Yeah," he said finally, voice low. "But look what it did to the place. And they thought it was okay."

Tom shrugged. "It was a different time."

Dan nodded faintly. "That's what worries me."

The others had already drifted toward the porch, voices low and easy as they stepped into the sun. But he stood there a moment longer, the photograph still echoing in his mind—the bare hills, the gouged earth, the thick ribbon of smoke threading through the valley like a scar.

It wasn't just what had happened. It was how ordinary it had seemed.

He turned from the image, stepping carefully down the creaking stairs.

Outside, Tom unlocked the car. Kira and Allison stood by the railing, looking down the street toward the saloon.

"Silver Dollar?" Tom asked.

Dan gave a small nod and followed them toward the car, but his thoughts stayed half a step behind. He kept seeing the treeless slope, the dead girl's folded hands, the way people had smiled through it all, convinced they were building something that would last.

The Silver Dollar Saloon looked like it had been lifted straight out of a sepia photograph—polished wood bar, pressed tin ceiling, walls cluttered with old signs and framed photographs of men in vests and narrow ties. A piano sat unused in the corner, keys yellowed with age.

They found a booth near the front windows, the Opera House across the street catching midday light on its ornate facade.

Tom slid into the bench seat and stretched his legs. "Can you imagine this place in the 1880s? Theater across the street, poker rooms behind every second door, silver money clinking in everyone's pocket."

Kira grinned. "And tuberculosis in every boarding house."

Allison laughed. "It wasn't all mines and survival, though. Some people really lived here. Opera, parties, little luxuries."

"Sure," Tom said. "If you'd already made your fortune. Or married it."

Their server came by, friendly and efficient, and left them with waters and menus thick with fried options and local pride.

As they settled in, Allison leaned a little toward Kira. "I meant to tell you, I've got an interview lined up in Boulder. Mara pulled some strings."

Kira raised her eyebrows, a glance flicking toward Dan before she caught herself. "Oh wow. That's exciting. How's that going to work?"

"Mara just moved down there," Allison said. "She's in a two-bedroom. If it works out, I could stay with her while I figure things out."

Kira nodded slowly. "And this is for that Basecamp job?"

"The title's assistant manager, but I'd be in charge of merchandise and purchasing." Allison said. "It's a big step up. Buying, seasonal planning, vendor relationships. Not just folding fleece jackets and straightening shelves."

Tom let out a low whistle. "Sounds like you're gunning for brand rep in a few years."

Allison shrugged but smiled. "If I want to stay in the industry, I've got to keep moving."

Dan didn't say anything. He was looking out the window at the Opera House across the street, its delicate arches and carved trim somehow untouched by the town's harder edges.

They stepped out into the afternoon light, the old storefronts of Main Street stretching ahead. The sidewalks were uneven in places, patched with concrete where old stone had cracked. Window displays mixed antique tools with tourist tchotchkes. Some shops were open, others shuttered with dusty signs still hanging in the glass. A little farther down, the Delaware Hotel stood in solemn profile—elegant but tired, its yellow brick façade faded by a hundred winters.

Kira slowed as they passed it. "I've always loved this building. Looks like it's waiting for something."

Tom snorted. "Waiting for a grant, maybe."

Allison looked up at the ornate balcony, the ironwork fine as lace. "Or a century to end."

They kept walking, the rhythm of their boots echoing softly down the block. There were people around, a couple heading into a gallery, someone unlocking a bike, but the town felt suspended, as if it hadn't decided whether it was coming back or slipping further into memory.

Dan glanced at the signs above the shops: Out West Books, Antique Row, Mountain Relics. Everything facing the past.

"This place..." he said gently. "It's not sure if it's going to make it."

Kira looked over at him.

He didn't mean the buildings. Not really.

"It might be stuck," he went on. "Forever in the echo of what it was."

No one disagreed. They just kept walking, past peeling paint and pride held together with time, the wind stirring faintly through banners left over from last summer's parade.

They reached the corner where the car was parked. Tom was already pulling out the keys, Kira checking her phone.

Allison lingered a step behind.

Dan glanced at her. She met his eyes for just a moment—steady, unreadable—then looked away.

He opened the passenger door and climbed in.

Behind them, Leadville stood quiet in the sun, its future curled somewhere beneath layers of wood and stone, waiting.

Ten

THE ROAD WIDENED as they dropped into the outskirts of Boulder, traffic thickening around them. The Flatirons stood like sentries as the town sprawled beneath—a web of bike lanes, roundabouts, and freshly painted crosswalks. Dan stayed in the right lane, watching for turns, trying not to grip the wheel.

Allison tapped the directions into her phone. "Take a left at the light on Canyon Boulevard."

He nodded, saying nothing.

Boulder felt bright. Charged—like a place that had figured something out and was waiting for the rest of the world to catch up. Cyclists passed them in tight packs, half of them looking like they could drop into the Tour de France any moment. cafes spilled onto the sidewalks. Buildings had modern lines and fresh paint, and every other billboard seemed to promise a better way to live.

They moved slowly as the traffic crawled, passing a co-op market, its chalkboard sign boasting of local honey, heritage grains, and elk sausage. A yoga studio above it had its windows wide open, people inside balanced like birds in the sun.

"I think we're close," Allison said. "It's just past the pedestrian bridge."

He merged right and eased the Tacoma into a small parking lot tucked behind a cluster of single-story buildings with glass fronts and natural wood trim. The Basecamp logo, mountains cut like a sawblade, was etched above the main entryway.

Allison checked the time. "Ten minutes early. That's good."

Dan turned off the motor. "Do you want me to wait here or...?"

"Looks like there's a coffee shop around the corner. I shouldn't be more than an hour."

He nodded, and she touched his arm briefly before stepping out, smoothing her shirt and slinging her leather bag over one shoulder. She paused in front of the building, squinting at its symmetry, then walked inside.

Dan watched the door swing shut behind her.

After a moment, he walked down the block to the cafe. The air was warmer on the front range than in the high mountains, dry and restless. Somewhere nearby, a dog barked, a kid yelled, and the city moved in small, steady patterns around him.

An hour passed, and then thirty more minutes before Dan looked up as the bell above the door chimed. Allison stepped into the cafe, eyes scanning until they landed on him near the window.

He stood as she crossed the room, brushing the hair from her face. "Hey," she said. "Sorry, the meeting ran a little long."

"No worries." He gestured to the cup in front of him. "You want a coffee? I can grab one."

She shook her head, already unzipping her jacket. "Actually, there's a place Mara told me about, just a few blocks up. Supposed to have great grain bowls and cold beer. Thought we could go there."

Dan hesitated for a second. "Yeah. Sure. Let me toss this."

He carried his cup to the trash while she adjusted the strap on her bag, already half-turned toward the door. She was flushed, an energy about her he hadn't seen in weeks.

Outside, the sidewalk was warm in the midday sun. A bus hissed to a stop down the block. People passed them in pairs, in motion.

"She says it's tucked behind a bookstore," Allison added. "Not much signage. One of those word-of-mouth places."

Dan offered a small smile. "Sounds like Boulder."

They started walking. He didn't ask how the interview had gone. Not yet. He could feel it in the way she moved—confident, slightly ahead of him on the sidewalk, as though she already knew the turns.

They sat at a shaded table tucked behind the little restaurant, plates pushed to the side. A few empty glasses caught the sun, casting dappled light across the tabletop. It was quiet, just the soft clink of silverware and the low murmur of a couple chatting nearby.

Allison set down her water glass, her expression thoughtful but steady. "So," she said. "Can I ask something we've both been avoiding?"

Dan looked up from the last bite of his sandwich. He didn't speak, but she took the silence as permission.

"If I get this job… what does that mean for us?"

He exhaled slowly and leaned back in his chair, eyes lifting to the string of lights strung across the cafe's courtyard. "I don't know."

"That's the thing," she said. "Neither do I. And I think… we're past the point where not knowing feels okay."

Dan nodded faintly but didn't meet her eyes. "You've got direction. I get that."

"And you don't?" she asked gently.

"I have… pieces. The job. The fieldwork. Whatever's happening to me out there. But it's not a plan. Not like this is, for you."

She let that sit for a moment. "I'm not asking you to follow me. Or to make a decision right this second. I just… I need to know if we're still moving together. Or if we're just moving?"

Dan glanced at her then, really looked, and saw not frustration, but clarity. Not a challenge, but a line gently drawn.

He wanted to say he didn't know. But something had loosened.

"I don't want to hold you back," he said, the words quiet and real.

"You're not," she replied. "But maybe we're just not in the same place anymore."

Dan nodded again. This time slower. "Yeah."

She didn't cry. Didn't reach for his hand. She just sat there, looking at him like someone watching a season change—no malice, no fight. Just the quiet certainty that something between them was now acknowledged.

The check came. Dan reached for it before her without a word.

The drive back passed quietly, the mountains rising again around them like a kind of shelter.

The front door creaked open and Shankley was already there, tail wagging, greeting them as if they'd returned from somewhere on the other side of the world.

"Hey, buddy," Dan said, stepping inside first. "Sorry we took so long."

Allison dropped her bag by the door and crouched to scratch behind Shankley's ears. "You okay, huh? Did you guard the place?"

He let out a soft, breathy woof and nosed her hand, then moved to Dan, circling once before trotting to the door and glancing back expectantly.

"Alright, alright," Dan mumbled, grabbing the leash from the hook. "Let's go."

He stepped back outside with the dog, the air cooler now the last light was settled behind the ridge. Shankley sniffed along the edge of the ditch, tail waving like none of it—Boulder, the silence in the car, the space widening between things—mattered much at all.

Dan followed, the leash loose in his hand, the dog leading him forward into the dusk.

Eleven

FALL CAME SLOWLY TO THE HIGH COUNTRY.

First in the mornings—the breath of frost on porch rails, the dog's ears lifting at sounds that hadn't mattered all summer. Then in the light, sharper at the edges, slanting lower across the ridgeline. Days still warmed, sometimes into the seventies, but the warmth felt softer now. As if the heat was borrowed. As if it might be called back without notice.

Down low, the ground cover had already started to turn with rust-colored leaves curling in the underbrush, the soft fade of green into ochre. Above them, the aspens were just beginning to catch up. A stitch of gold here and there, subtle as breath, working its way into the canopy.

A quiet had settled over the forest trails, the birds almost silent, the wildflowers gone to seed. The air carried the dry weight of old pine and the faint sweetness of fallen leaves.

It was that short window the mountains gave you every year, a second-chance summer. No guarantees. Just a stretch of days that felt like forgiveness.

The porch boards were cool beneath his feet, steam from his mug curling into pale air. Dan stood just outside the open door, one hand around the coffee, the other tucked into his sweatshirt pocket. The ridge caught the first light like always—slow and deliberate, a warm bleed across the peaks.

Shankley lay stretched out on the porch beside him, chin resting on his paws, an ear raised and twitching.

"Pretty nice," Dan grunted, voice low and rough with sleep. "Not bad at all."

The dog gave him a side-eye in vague agreement.

Dan took another sip. The coffee was no longer hot, but he didn't mind. Mornings like this didn't ask much of him. He liked that. The quiet. The smallness of it.

"Gonna check trailheads today," he said, more to himself than anything. "Figure we'll take the long loop; the trailheads are packed with hunters already. Good chance to check tags and see who's out early."

Shankley didn't move, but Dan saw the ear twitch at the word "loop."

He looked out over the clearing. The brush at the edge had dulled, the low thickets rusted with change. A few birds flitted tree to tree, silent and fast, already busy with whatever it was they knew to do before snow came.

Dan sipped again, the mug still warming his hands. Behind him, the house stood quiet. No kettle whistling. No second cup waiting.

He leaned against the porch rail and watched a single yellow leaf break loose from the nearest aspen, spiraling down through the morning air.

"Won't be long now," he murmured.

Shankley rose and stretched, spine bowed, tongue curling in a lazy yawn.

Dan nodded. "Alright, buddy. Let's get moving."

The field office sat quiet in the early light, the sun just catching the top of the radio tower as Dan pulled in. Sean's truck was already there, and Dan parked beside it and killed the engine.

Inside, the lights were on. A coffee pot hissed and clicked on the counter. Sean stood at the whiteboard, capping a marker, while Ken stood close to the coffee pot, empty mug swinging impatiently.

"Mornin'," Dan said as he stepped through the door, Shankley trailing just behind before curling up in his usual spot near the heater vent.

Sean glanced over his shoulder. "You're late," he said, deadpan.

Dan checked his watch. "By about four minutes."

Sean shrugged. "That's how it starts."

Ken looked up. "If this crew ever started on time, I'd call the papers."

Dan grabbed a mug and jumped into line behind Ken. "I was planning on checking trailheads today. Make sure folks are tagged up, see who's coming out with meat."

Ken grunted. "Yeah. The start of hunting season—too early for snow, too late for common sense."

The room settled for a moment, the comfortable silence of people who'd done a lot of mornings together.

The radio crackled to life on the shelf behind Ken. He turned halfway, glancing at the frequency.

"Dispatch, Eagle Field Office," came the voice—slightly fuzzy, but clear enough.

Ken crossed the room and picked up the handset. "Go ahead."

"Caller reporting up Squaw Creek," dispatch said. "Homeowner's hit a deer in their driveway late last night. Says the animal's still there this morning. Possibly a broken leg."

Ken met Dan's eyes, then pressed the button again. "Did the caller say how close they got?"

"Not clear. Said the deer's limping badly. Still mobile but not leaving the property."

Ken clicked off and set the handset down gently. He didn't speak right away.

Dan finished the last of his coffee and set the mug in the sink. "I can check it."

Ken nodded slowly. "Yeah. It could be a spooked yearling working out a bruise or it could be a compound fracture."

He rubbed a hand across his jaw. "You're headed that direction anyway. Why don't you take a look?"

"Sure," Dan murmured.

Ken's voice stayed level, but there was a weight in it now. "If it's bad, you'll know."

Dan gave a small nod and turned back toward the door, Shankley already on his feet, tail twitching.

* * *

The gravel gave way to patchy asphalt as Dan turned off the main road, following the narrow lane that led toward the Squaw Creek property. It curved through stands of thinning aspen, the trees taller here, the light broken into flickers. He noticed a wooden mailbox with peeling paint marking the drive. He slowed, scanning ahead.

The cabin came into view, set back beneath a rise, roofline tucked low like it didn't want to be noticed. A few outbuildings flanked it—a small shed, a covered woodpile, a carport where a silver SUV sat angled like it had been parked in a hurry.

Dan pulled in behind it and killed the engine. The place was quiet. Not silent, but a kind of quiet that lived out here—wind in the trees, the dry rustle of leaves, a jay somewhere off to his right letting out a sharp call.

The front door opened before he could step out. A woman in her sixties waved from the porch.

"He's still here," she called down. "Back behind the shed. I saw him this morning, lying in the same spot."

Dan nodded and got out, giving a short command for Shankley to stay put. He crossed the yard slowly, not yet reaching for the gear in the back.

"Are you the one who hit it?" he asked, voice calm.

She grimaced. "Didn't even see him. It came down the drive and he just—stepped into it. I thought I missed him, but then this morning I saw him limping. Real bad."

Dan followed her gesture toward the back of the property.

"Alright," he said. "I'll take a look."

He moved with purpose, measured strides that landed quietly on his toes. Behind the shed, the land sloped gently toward the creek, choked with brush and golden grass. It didn't take long to spot the deer.

It stood partway in the brush, one hind leg lifted and dangling. It wasn't running. Just watching.

Dan crouched slowly, not getting too close. He took in the angle of the leg, the way the animal kept shifting its weight but never settled.

"Damn," he murmured.

Dan took another step forward, slow and deliberate, watching the deer's chest move in shallow, rapid breaths. Its ears flicked once, and for a moment he thought it might stay.

Then it turned.

The motion wasn't graceful. The injured leg hung like a rope behind it, but the front half of the body surged into motion, and that was enough. It crashed into the brush, scattering leaves and snapping twigs, gone before Dan could shift his weight to follow.

"Shit."

He stood still for a moment, taking in the silence. No birdsong. Just the soft rattle of branches where it had passed.

Dan moved into the brush, careful, eyes scanning low. He found the start of a trail easily by the flattened grass and dark smear on a rock edge. After twenty minutes of slow tracking, the trail just ended. The deer had veered toward the creek, maybe crossed it, maybe not. The prints faded. The blood, if it had been blood, dried invisible.

He stood for a while in the shallows, boots planted on cold stone, watching the water slip past.

The deer still had enough fight in it to disappear. He hoped it was enough to matter.

Dan circled for another ten minutes, cutting a slow arc along the creek, but the trail was gone. Either the deer had crossed water or vanished into thicker cover. Either way, he'd lost it.

He made his way back up through the brush, boots snagging on dry roots, burrs catching in his pant legs. The sun had lifted higher now, filtering gold through the aspen as he stepped into the yard again.

The woman stood on the porch, arms folded. She didn't say anything—just raised her eyebrows slightly.

Dan gave a small shake of his head. "It disappeared but it's still mobile. Best case, it heals."

"And worst?"

He glanced back toward the trees. "Nature takes its course."

She nodded once, then turned and went inside.

Dan opened the truck door, and Shankley jumped down to meet him, sniffing at his boots like he already knew the answer. Dan scratched behind the dog's ears and climbed in, dust rising beneath the tires as he rolled back down the drive.

The radio popped once as he came around the bend. Ken's voice crackled through.

"Did you get a look at the deer?"

"Briefly, it didn't hold still long. I lost it."

There was a pause.

"Nothing to be done," Ken said.

Dan looked out toward the ridgeline as it slipped past the passenger window. "Not today."

He set the handset back in the cradle and let the silence ride the rest of the way down.

TWELVE

DAN MOVED SLOWLY along the narrow game path, ducking beneath a low-slung pine limb, brushing aside the dead weight of fir boughs as he passed. Shankley trotted just ahead, his blaze-orange vest catching flashes of light through the thinning canopy. The wind had picked up around midday and hadn't let go. Now it gusted fitfully, pushing through standing timber, the tops of trees moving carelessly.

Most of the leaves lay on the ground. What clung to the aspens came in patches—shriveled scraps of gold, black-spotted and dry. The understory had turned sodden and colorless, and the duff underfoot brown and black, melded as one. Each step gave off the smell of softened bark, of rot beginning.

They were deep into the Red and White. Not designated wilderness, just wild country that didn't offer much of a reason to come looking unless you were chasing elk or trying to disappear.

Dan adjusted the strap of his pack and paused to catch his breath. His legs ached from the climb and the miles. The dog turned to look back at him, ears perked, waiting without expectation.

"Hold up," Dan said. "Let an old man rest a second."

Shankley dropped to a crouch, tongue lolling.

Dan pulled his beanie down tighter and looked out across the slope. Pines leaned eastward, shaped by years of snow loading heavy on their windward sides, the sky above them sharpening toward evening. It was late enough in the year that even good days ended early.

He hadn't seen a hunter since mid-morning. Just the odd track in the mud, and once, remains of guts from a hunter's kill, partially scavenged by the coyotes, the leavings beginning to rot.

They picked up again. Dan stepped over a fallen log slick with lichen, boots careful on the damp bark.

Shankley moved slower now too, staying close, alert and ears twitching at nothing in particular. The dog paused once to nose at a tangle of fur snagged on a stump—old, grey, maybe elk. Dan crouched to take a closer look, but there was nothing fresh. Just the trace of something already gone.

He stood again, stretched his back, and turned toward the ridgeline.

That's when it came.

A single, distant crack.

Sharp and flat, carried on the wind from somewhere far off—far enough to be harmless, but close enough to feel wrong.

Dan froze.

Shankley stopped mid-step, head turning toward the sound, muscles coiled.

There was nothing after it. No echo. No follow-up shot. Just the slow groan of the wind moving through bare branches.

Dan scanned the slope below. Nothing moved.

Too late in the day for a shot that far back. Too far out for someone to be taking chances.

He reached down and rested his hand on Shankley's back.

The dog was still staring into the trees.

Dan remained unmoving.

The crack had echoed behind his ribs long after the air had gone quiet. It wasn't just the sound, but the way it landed. Flat. Final. Like a door slamming in a house you thought was empty.

Dan scanned the ridge. Nothing. No movement. No second shot. Just the soundless aftermath, the forest closing in again like it had never been interrupted.

"Let's go," he said, but the words came out softer than he meant. Like speaking too loud might bring something into view.

They moved slowly uphill, off the faint track now, into a stand of pine where the light struggled to reach. Branches scratched gently across his sleeves. The air felt thinner here; cooler, more metallic.

Then he smelled it.

Not blood. Not animal.

Earth. Damp and raw, like the first breath after a storm. The sharp scent of mineral soil turning under itself.

He paused again, this time without knowing why.

The ground didn't look different, but something in it had changed. He could feel it pressing up through the soles of his boots—cool, insistent. The way presence feels when you don't see it but know it's there.

Shankley turned to him. No sound. Just a look, sharp and waiting.

Dan's chest tightened.

And something inside him shifted—not forward, not back.

Just... out.

The smell deepened.

It wasn't coming from the ground anymore—it *was* the ground. It filled his head, his mouth, coated his tongue with something rich and damp and undeniable.

His knees buckled, not from pain, not quite from exhaustion. It was something else. A loosening. The pressure in his limbs felt strange. Like they didn't belong to him.

He reached out to steady himself against a pine, but his hand didn't quite land right. Or maybe it wasn't a hand anymore.

He was breathing hard now. The wind came sharper and colder. But it wasn't wind anymore, it was *scent*. A thousand threads of meaning: fox urine, distant elk, the faint electric tang of metal rubbed into boot leather. Every breath told him something.

His ears rang once, then cleared.

The world opened wide.

He blinked, but the lids didn't feel like his own. Vision stretched outward—shallower, broader. The trees rearranged themselves. Shadows deepened into paths and light fractured into motion.

Somewhere, the part of him that had a name still *knew*. Still understood what was happening.

But it was getting quiet now.

That part was getting very, very quiet.

He stood still on the slope, four legs grounded to the earth, lungs drawing in the world one scent at a time. Head high, ears flicking, every muscle ready to move. The orange vest was gone.

The forest didn't care.

He was just another thing that belonged.

He moved through the trees without sound.

The weight of the body felt right. Heavy in the chest, strong in the flanks. Each hoofstep landed with quiet certainty, the way water shapes to stone. The forest welcomed him—not with warmth, but with belonging. He was not new here. Only returned.

The air was full of pine, fox tracks, and owl feathers. The sweet rot of fallen aspen. Everything layered and sharp.

And then, faintly, something else.

He stopped.

Stillness settled over his body like snow. One hoof suspended. Breath held. Ears angled.

There it was again.

The scent of man.

Distant, but close enough to matter. A shape in the wind. A heat beneath bark. Not moving. Not near. But *wrong*.

He stayed that way a long time. Motionless. His heart slowed to match the forest's pace but the man didn't come closer.

But he was there. Somewhere below, or across the ridge, or carried up on the wrong kind of breeze. A thing made of noise and oil and metal.

The buck turned.

He stepped lightly over a patch of windblown needles, angled down toward a break in the trees. The air carried something bitter and acrid. A tang that didn't belong.

The man was close.

He couldn't see him, but he *felt* him. His coiled breath, the tight stillness of something that watched. That waited.

The buck froze.

Every muscle locked. Ears forward. Chest taut. His own breath a danger.

The wind shifted.

And then it came.

A sharp crack. Closer than the first. The bark behind him exploded in a burst of splinters and dust. The sound rolled through him—not just noise but impact, pressure, the violent tearing of air.

He ran.

With no thought, no direction. Only speed. Legs driving forward, hooves crashing over stone, brush, shallow ditch. No path. No pattern. Just away.

Trees blurred past. His lungs burned. But he didn't stop.

Not until the scent was gone, the sound was gone, and the forest finally stilled again.

Dan slowly opened his eyes.

He was on his knees.

The forest spun around him, colorless and grainy. His sweatshirt clung to his back with sweat. His hand was pressed flat to the earth.

He couldn't move right away.

His body remembered something his mind hadn't caught up to.

The shot. The tearing air. The blind panic.

He sat back slowly, breath ragged, stomach tight.

It wasn't the sound that undid him. It was the *feeling*.

The raw, animal certainty that death was seconds away and that he had no control, no words, no shelter. Only fear.

Not fear like he'd ever known.

This had no name. No story. Just fire in the veins and the scream of a body trying to stay alive.

He sat like that for a long time, staring at the place where the sun had fallen.

And didn't speak a word.

Thirteen

THE WORLD HAD GONE STILL.

Still but not peaceful.

Paused, like it was waiting to see what came next.

Snow had settled in for good, crusted in layers along the roadside, banks pushed high by the county plows. The trees wore it quietly, white clinging to their shaded sides like an afterthought. Even the sun, when it came, felt distant. Pale and angled, like it had no intention to stay.

Dan woke in darkness most mornings. Not early—just still dark. The darkness that stretched too long, so when light finally did come, it felt like a mistake. He rose slowly, joints stiff, breath clouding the cold air above the covers. The little house was quiet, colder than it should be. The heater kicked in late most mornings, coughing through the vents like it had to think about it first.

Shankley padded across the floor when he heard Dan stir, tail sweeping the cold boards. He didn't whine—just waited, the way he always had. Loyal, but restless. He didn't understand the stillness. Not really. He just knew something had changed.

Dan sat on the edge of the bed and rubbed his face, brushing sleep aside. Outside, the ridge was still dark, its outline just beginning to separate from the sky. The bedroom light cast a faint glow across the snowdrifts, untouched since yesterday's storm. No tracks. No sound. Just the quiet of a world tucked in too tight.

He pulled on a sweatshirt and socks and padded into the kitchen. The kettle was already half-full from the night before. He clicked it on and waited, eyes unfocused, breath steaming faintly in the chill.

There were days now when he didn't say anything before noon. Not out of mood, exactly. Just... because. The silence had stretched itself around him like the snow—soft at first, then weighty.

He poured an instant coffee and stepped onto the porch. Shankley followed, settling beside Dan like always. But he didn't lie down.

The dog stood watchful, ears twitching at sounds only he could hear.

Dan looked out over the yard. The brush had vanished under snow. The road hadn't been plowed. Tire tracks from yesterday were already filled. The winter hush that came this time of year—sound muffled by snow, distance collapsed.

He took a sip. The coffee burned just a little, but he didn't mind.

The change hadn't come again since the buck.

It hadn't disappeared altogether. Not exactly. It was still there, somewhere under the skin. Like a tick in his blood or a muscle that wouldn't unclench.

He hadn't told anyone. Not Sean. Not Ken.

What could he say, anyway? That he'd felt the world rearrange itself around him. That he'd run on hooves through the trees and known, for a moment, exactly what it was to be prey?

He couldn't even explain it to himself.

Shankley let out a low whuff, not quite a bark. Just enough to remind the world they were still here.

Dan reached down and rubbed the dog's shoulder. "I know, buddy."

The sky was paling now—blue bleeding up from the ridge, soft and slow. The wind was starting to rise too, brushing through the branches with a dry rattle.

Winter had locked the backcountry down. No more field hikes. No more trailhead rounds. Just office calls, paperwork, the occasional dispatch. The quiet followed him home.

And in it, he was starting to feel something unfamiliar.

Not grief or guilt, but a quiet shift in gravity. Like his weight had moved, and he hadn't noticed when.

Dan finished his coffee, then stood.

The cold had crept into his legs. He stretched once and stepped back inside. Shankley followed, nails clicking lightly across the floor.

He layered up grabbing his long sleeve, old fleece, and the heavier coat, the gloves from the cubby by the door. The snow wasn't deep, just the soft kind that fell in the night—enough to hide the old drifts, to make the world look clean again.

Still, it needed moving.

He grabbed the shovel from its usual place and leaned beside the porch rail. There were two of them—

his and hers, though one hadn't been used in months. He grabbed the red handle without thinking. It had always been hers.

He took it now because it no longer mattered.

She was gone.

The first scrape of metal against wood echoed sharper than he expected. The world so quiet he'd forgotten how loud it could be. Shankley stood at the edge of the porch, watching him, then dropped down into the yard, nosing at the snow near the woodpile.

Dan worked in slow rows—porch first, then the short path to the drive. It didn't need to be perfect. No one was coming. But still he carved out the edges, squared the corners, made it look right. The way she used to like it.

She'd never said much, just had a way of looking at things when they were left half-done. Not judgment, exactly. Just... disappointment. Or maybe that was just how it landed on him.

It didn't matter now. Boulder had happened. And he wasn't chasing that shadow anymore.

Still—

He cleared all the way to the road.

Dan slipped back inside and Shankley was already watching him.

"Alright," Dan whispered softly. "Let's go."

The leash hung untouched by the door and he didn't take it. Around town, Shankley stayed close.

They stepped into the cold, boots and paws crunching across the driveway where wind had started to drift fine snow back into the path he'd just cleared. Dan didn't bother fixing it.

The road into town was mostly empty. One truck passed, tires humming on the packed snow, and the driver lifted two fingers from the wheel. Dan nodded back. A small-town courtesy. Nothing behind it but routine.

They walked without purpose, just a loop through the familiar. The river curved beyond the edge of the road, its surface half-frozen, grey and silent.

Dan watched it slip beneath a low bridge, slow and steady.

He thought again about the transformations that lived somewhere beneath the surface, like that river—partially covered, always moving.

He tried not to name them in his head, but they came anyway.

The crow.

The rabbit.

The buck.

Not just memories, but something more. Impressions that didn't belong to him. Reflexes that had nothing to do with his human body. Sounds and scents and angles of light that still showed up in dreams—or worse, in the middle of the day, when everything was quiet.

Sometimes he'd walk past a stretch of road and feel the urge to take flight. Not metaphorically. His shoulders would tighten like wings trying to lift. Or he'd freeze, just for a second, every muscle gone still like prey.

He hadn't told anyone. Of course he hadn't.

Because how do you say that out loud?

That you ran through the trees on hooves. That you smelled metal before you heard the shot. That your eyes still search the dark for shadows that belong to a world not yours.

That sometimes, with his eyes closed, he still saw the world the way they did—broad and split, everything happening at once.

They turned past the edge of town, where the snow piled higher against old fences and the mailboxes leaned at odd angles. Shankley nosed at a drift and sneezed.

Dan stopped. Hands in his pockets, breath rising in soft puffs.

He didn't feel scared. Not exactly. But it was changing him. That much was clear. It wasn't just the act of shifting, but the part that stayed.

The instincts.

The quiet.

The knowing.

He looked up at the ridge beyond the rooftops. The forest beyond it.

Still frozen. Still waiting.

And finally, the thought came—clean, sharp, and impossible to put away.

It wasn't just becoming the animal. It was the lingering knowledge that came back with him.

* * *

Someone had tracked in slush that melted into dirty puddles across the entry tile of the Field Office. The heater kicked on with a low rattle as Dan stepped inside, knocking snow from his boots.

Shankley shook off behind him, then settled near the vent as always. Creature of habit.

Sean was leaning against the file cabinet near the window, half-watching the snowfall, half-peeling the label off a bottle of seltzer. He turned when the door opened.

"Look who survived the deep freeze," he said. "I figured you were out back teaching your dog Morse code with tail wags."

Dan cracked half a smile, but it didn't quite reach his eyes. He tugged off his gloves and stuffed them in his coat pocket.

Ken looked up from his desk. He didn't say anything right away, just watched Dan a moment longer than usual.

"How's it going?" Sean asked, not unkind. Just... easy. The way men asked when they didn't want to push.

Dan shrugged. "Just tired. Long week."

Ken didn't look away. He leaned back in his chair, arms crossed.

"You probably wouldn't be interested in this," he'd said. "But something came across my desk."

Ken's voice was level.

"A temporary placement. Spring through fall in Yellowstone. Someone's retired and they need a body. Someone with a wildlife background. Your name came up."

Dan glanced over, brow raised.

Ken's voice was level. "Someting you might think about."

Dan gave a small snort, mostly to buy time. "Montana, it's colder up there than it is here."

"Yeah," Sean said. "A National Park, protected wildlife. Doesn't sound like you at all."

Dan let the jab pass.

Ken didn't press. Just nodded slightly, like he was putting something away for later.

The radio cracked faintly in the corner. No one moved to answer it right away.

Outside, snow began to fall again—light and dry, whispering against the windows.

Dan stayed at the office later than he meant to. Not doing much other than shuffling through reports, half-reading an old memo, and fixing the fuel log that Sean had messed up again. Nothing that mattered, but enough to look busy.

The others had cleared out an hour ago. Sean with a joke about frozen burritos, Ken with a nod and his usual quiet exit.

Dan stayed until the room emptied out, until the light outside had shifted from gray to nearly gone.

He didn't like going home lately. Not because of anything there. Just the silence and the way it settled too fast—too full, like it had been waiting for him.

He finally locked up, pointing the truck back towards home, headlights cutting wide arcs over the snowbanks. The drive settled him and Shankley moved closer as they fell into the rhythm of the trip.

Dan parked in his usual spot and killed the engine. The heater ticked as it cooled.

He didn't move right away.

Instead, he sat in the dark cab and let the silence fill in around him.

He was still doing the job. Still getting out into the field, still filing his reports.

But people talked at him and he answered, like he was moving through it all a half-step behind.

He didn't know what it was yet—not fully. But he could feel it.

Ken had seen it. So had Sean, in his way. Hell, even Shankley had.

Dan exhaled slowly, breath fogging the windshield. The world didn't feel wrong. It just didn't feel *like his* anymore.

He sat in the truck until the heater went cold.

The sky outside was dark and filled with stars. He stayed.

Not because he was lost.

But because something in him had already begun to leave.

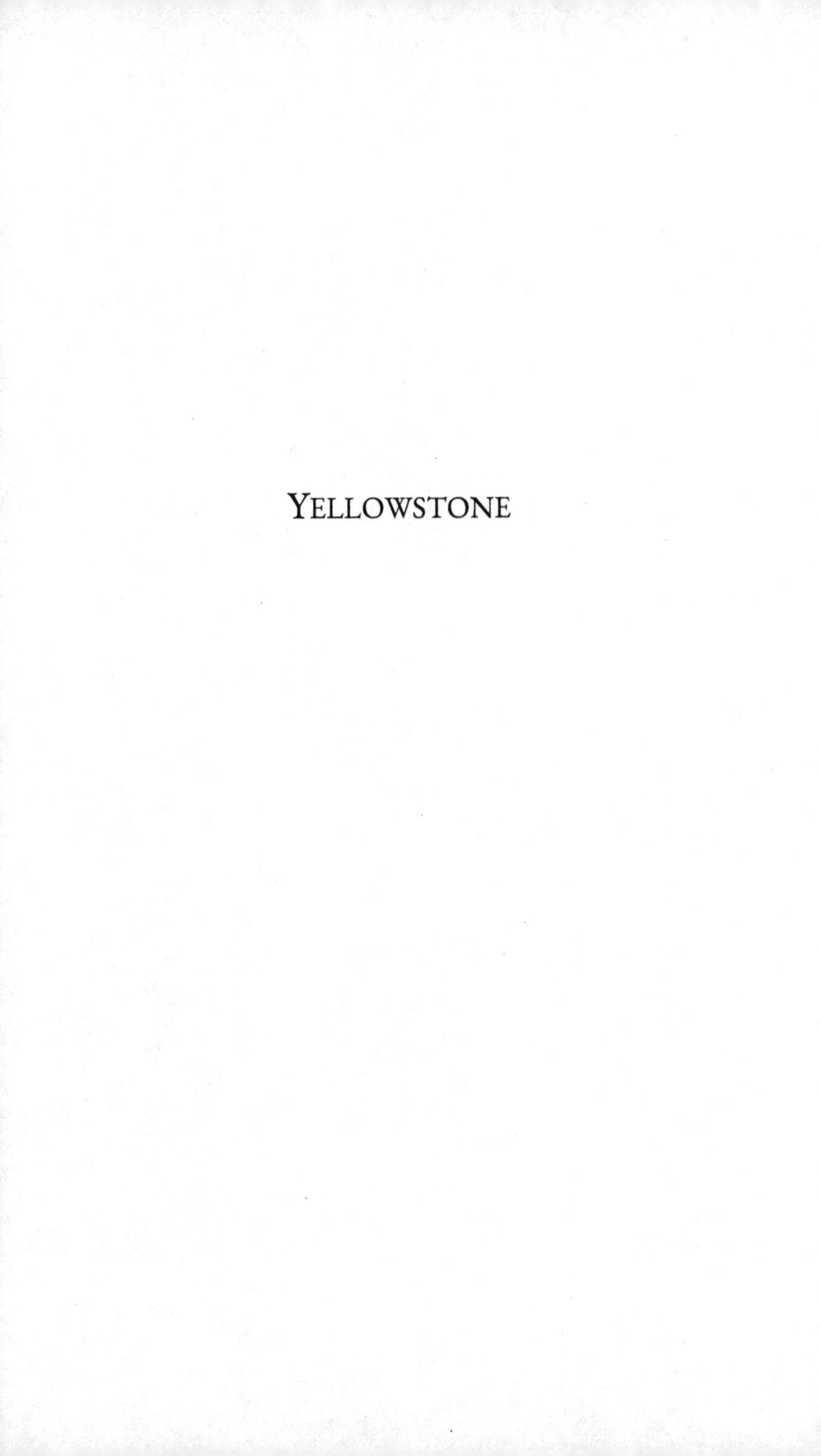

Yellowstone

FOURTEEN

DAN CRESTED THE FINAL RISE JUST AFTER NOON. The snow was nearly gone now—just streaks in the shade, giving way to dirt and the start of spring. Then the park opened up beneath him—hills tight with sagebrush, stands of aspen just beginning to bud, and beyond it all, the steaming terraces that marked Mammoth.

He pulled over for a moment, engine idling. Shankley sat up, nose working hard to understand the unfamiliar.

Dan took a breath. Not awed, but... Yellowstone.

He drove down into it slowly. Through the gate, past a ranger shack, then along the curve of the administrative buildings—stone and timber, flat-roofed. A few people walked in jackets and caps, headed somewhere with purpose.

Rita Matsuda, his new supervisor, had given him directions to employee housing. A low beige building tucked back near a thicket of bare cottonwoods. One unit on the end had a number taped to the door. He pulled in and cut the engine.

Dan got out, stretched, and looked around. A raven flapped overhead, then perched on a roof vent across the lot. It watched him with lazy confidence.

He let Shankley out. The dog padded across the lot, nose to ground, then froze with his head turned, ears sharp.

Dan followed his gaze for a second, then shook it off. "It's yours too now," he said softly, almost smiling.

He keyed in the access code and pushed on the door which resisted at first. It was tight in the frame and creaky in the hinges. The place smelled faintly of old carpet and industrial cleaner, but it was warm, and a low radiator hummed along the far wall.

A single bed, a desk, and a worn loveseat pushed beneath the window. There was a corkboard above the desk with a note pinned to it in neat handwriting with black ink.

> Dan—
>
> Welcome to Yellowstone. Come by my office tomorrow morning when you're settled. 8:30 is fine. —Rita

No orientation packet, no formal welcome. Just the note, the heat, and the view through the window—rivulets of snowmelt winding down the hill like spilled thread.

Dan dropped his bag inside the door and stood for a moment, not moving. It wasn't much. But it didn't have to be.

He stepped out onto the stoop and watched the sky for a time. Pale blue, wide open—Dan was beginning to understand what that actually meant.

That night, Dan dreamed of wind.

A wind that raised him. He felt the motion—fast and rising. Land flashing beneath him, wide and dark. He felt the wings he couldn't see. The pull of air against bone and feathers.

He woke before dawn. The dreams wouldn't leave him, even here. But he was learning not to fight them.

Shankley was curled up at the foot of the bed. He raised his head then pulled tighter, falling instantly back into sleep.

Dan sat for a while before getting up, making coffee, and pulling on his boots.

The administrative offices were tucked in a long, low building across from the visitor center. Dan stepped inside and found everything just as he'd expected from someone like Rita—orderly, quiet, no clutter. No frills, no bulletin board full of old flyers. Just a clean front desk, neatly labeled forms, and a single framed map of the park.

The woman at the desk looked up. Mid-forties, park-issued fleece, composed.

"You're the Colorado guy," she said, not asking.

"Dan Nowak."

She stood to shake his hand. "Jillian. Rita's in her office. You're early."

"Yeah, that's a habit."

She gave a small nod and held his gaze for a moment—not unfriendly, just weighing him.

"You're not a rookie. That'll go a long way around here. The rookies always want Yellowstone."

Dan offered the ghost of a shrug. "I like the fieldwork best."

That earned the faintest smile. "She'll want to hear that."

Jillian tapped the door lightly and opened it without waiting.

Jillian stepped aside. "Rita? He's here."

Dan followed her in.

The office was spare but purposeful—window cracked an inch, a clean desk, a laptop open, and a large topo map of the northern range marked up with colored pins. Rita Matsuda stood behind the desk, closing a field notebook.

"Dan Nowak," she said, as if confirming something already settled.

"That's me."

"You're early."

"I don't like being late."

"Good," she said. "Let's keep it that way."

She motioned to the chair. Dan sat.

"I heard you had a four-legged partner back in Colorado."

"I still do," Dan said. "Shankley. He's with me."

Rita's expression didn't change, but there was the flicker of a grin in her eyes.

"Well, he's not on the payroll here. I've got a two-legged guy lined up to get you going, Wyatt Keller. He knows the northern range better than most."

She pulled a folder from her desk and slid it across. "Radio codes, maps, gate sheets. There's a training video in there if you enjoy wasting your time. Wyatt will cover what matters."

Dan opened the folder, glanced at the top sheet. Clean layout with everything in order.

"You can ride with him the next week or two," Rita continued. "Learn the land, the people, where grizzlies sleep and tourists get lost. After that, I'll figure out where you're most useful."

"Fair enough."

"Ken says you're steady," she said. "That you don't leave a mess, and you don't whine when cleaning up someone else's."

"I know the work."

"That's what we need."

She leaned back slightly, finally letting the moment ease.

"Welcome to Yellowstone, Nowak."

Rita dismissed him with a nod, already turning back to her laptop.

Jillian handed him a key card and directions to the uniform room—basement level, down the hall, first door on the left. He thanked her and made his way down, boots echoing against the old tile floor.

The uniform room was unstaffed. Just shelves, hangers, and a clipboard for sign-outs. Dan found the basics in his size: trousers, field shirt, fleece vest, the green-and-tan color scheme that hadn't changed in decades. He held up the iconic Yellowstone Ranger hat, then left it on the shelf. One step at a time.

Back at his unit, he changed in front of the mirror over the small sink. The shirt was stiff with starch. The patch on the sleeve looked official, even if he didn't feel it yet.

For a second, catching his reflection, he smirked.

"Ranger Smith," he muttered. "Watch out for bears."

Shankley thumped his tail against the floor, unimpressed.

Dan turned from the mirror, buttoned the last button, and rolled his shoulders into the new outfit.

That afternoon, he took a walk.

The day had warmed slightly, enough to melt the last of the snow from the walkways. He left his fleece unzipped and let the sun do what it could. Shankley trotted alongside, tail up, alert but relaxed. A few other staff crossed paths with them, one nodded, one didn't, but no one stopped him.

Mammoth was quiet. A few government buildings, a scattering of houses tucked into the slope, the old parade ground still ringed with split-rail fencing. Steam drifted up from the terraces to the south, hanging in the breeze like breath.

He followed a paved trail past the edge of the upper springs. Shankley stopped to drink from a shallow puddle, then kept going, ears pivoting toward something in the trees. Dan stood still, letting the sulfur and sage settle into his nose. The air was different here—drier, sharper, with a hint of mineral. It felt like something old just under the surface.

He passed a sign for Liberty Cap, the stub of an ancient cone rising like a fossilized chimney. There were hoof prints in the soft dirt beside the path—elk, maybe bison. This wasn't wilderness, not exactly, but the wild wasn't far.

He looped around toward the edge of the staff housing complex. A pair of mule deer stood in the shade of a lodgepole pine, watching him without alarm. Shankley saw them but stayed close, well-trained and well-traveled.

Dan gave a small nod, more to himself than anything else.

FIFTEEN

DAN STOOD ON THE STEPS outside the ranger office, collar zipped high, hands buried in his jacket pockets. Early spring smelled faintly of sulfur. Steam drifted from the terraces across the road.

A door opened behind him. "Are you Dan Novak?"

Dan turned. The man was broad-shouldered and gray-stubbled, a baseball cap pulled low and wraparound sunglasses.

"It's Nowak," Dan replied. "O sounds like 'go.'"

The man squinted. "That right?" Then he held out a hand. "Wyatt Keller."

Dan shook it. Wyatt's grip was dry, strong, and brief.

"Boss says I'm babysitting you this week. Lucky me." Wyatt started down the steps. "Truck's this way."

Dan followed without a word. The government vehicle was already warming, the beat of the diesel thumping steadily in the morning stillness. A pair of elk grazed beside the dormitory parking lot. One raised its head and stared at them as they passed, its breath pluming in the cold.

Wyatt gestured with his chin. "Those two have been hanging around since March. They think they own the place."

Dan nodded, resisting the urge to reach for his phone and snap a shot.

They climbed in. Dan slid the thermos onto the jump seat in back.

"No dog?" Wyatt asked as he shifted into drive.

"Left him in housing," Dan replied, unsure if this was some kind of test. "I figured I'd wait to see how far the rules can get bent around here."

Wyatt grunted. "Smart move. Rita's old-school."

They turned out of Mammoth, winding slowly uphill. The thermal terraces passed in a blur of steam, muted blues and whites. A crow flapped past the windshield, wings flashing silver in the early light.

Neither man spoke for a while. The road climbed, then leveled, opening onto a high meadow where the grass held the color of old straw. A few bison dotted the hillsides, dark and slow-moving against the pale slope. One stood in the middle of the road. Wyatt eased to a stop.

The bison blinked once, then lowered its head slightly. Not a threat—just indifferent to the truck.

"Don't honk," Wyatt said flatly. "It just pisses them off."

They waited. Dan watched the bison's flank rise and fall, a steady rhythm. There was something about the animal that went beyond calm—it didn't yield. It belonged.

"I could watch that all day," Dan murmured.

Wyatt didn't respond at first. Then: "Most people are just in a hurry to get past."

The bison moved eventually, stepping off the pavement with no urgency at all. Wyatt rolled forward, and the truck crested the next ridge.

Ahead, the road stretched toward Tower Junction, and beyond that, the wide open of Lamar Valley.

Dan sat back in his seat. Something in his chest had let go. He exhaled; slow and quiet, and let the day begin.

They passed Blacktail Plateau without speaking. Wyatt kept one hand on the wheel, the other resting loosely on the window ledge, gloved fingers tapping out a quiet rhythm against the door. Every so often, he'd offer a nod toward a coyote in the sagebrush, or a hawk lifted by thermals, but he didn't name things, didn't explain.

Dan appreciated the silence. It left space to notice wildlife on a scale he'd never seen before.

A small herd of pronghorn flared white across a distant ridge. A stand of fire-scarred pines clawed upward from a blackened slope. Yellowstone didn't need to be picturesque. It didn't need to pose. It just was.

Wyatt finally spoke as they came around a bend and dropped into the flats. "We'll stop up at Slough. Check the board, maybe catch a glimpse if we're lucky."

Dan nodded. "Wolves?"

"Yeah. Junction Butte pack. They den back in the draw. Tourists'll start clogging up the lot by June, but for now it's just the lifers, the loonies, and us."

He pulled into a turnout already dotted with a few scopes and some folding chairs. A scattering of bundled figures clustered at the edge of the overlook, long lenses pointed east.

"Grab your binocs," Wyatt said. "I'll do the talking."

Dan followed him out into the chill. The wind tugged at his collar. Someone had chalked sightings on the metal signboard: *alpha female seen near den 06:12, four pups active, one black-phase male northeast slope.*

They stood for a while without speaking. A man in a down vest whispered something to a woman wrapped in a blanket, but most people just watched.

Then, there was movement. A dark blur along the tree line. Then another.

Dan raised his binoculars.

Three wolves loped across the clearing beyond the draw—lean, swift, at home. One paused to sniff the air, then trotted on. A smaller one, likely a yearling, gave chase to something unseen, darting through a patch of low willows before vanishing behind a rise.

Dan lowered the glasses. The cold had sunk through his jacket, but he barely felt it. The stillness was back—a feeling of presence. The land hummed under everything.

"You all right?" Wyatt asked, almost casually.

Dan nodded. "Yeah. Just—taking it in."

Wyatt didn't smile, but something softened in his posture. "First time's a punch in the gut," he said. "Next time it's worse."

Dan almost asked what he meant. But the words didn't come. They stood together a little longer, shoulder to shoulder, watching wolves move through a world that didn't care who was watching.

Eventually, Wyatt tipped his head toward the truck. "Let's move, there's more to see."

Dan turned once more toward the valley before following him.

The road bent east, curving gently downhill. As they rounded a low ridge, the land unfolded all at once—wide, layered, open.

Lamar Valley.

To the left, the river traced a pale ribbon through the flats, ice still hanging on in the shadows. Beyond that, hills rolled outward, their tops dusted with snow.

Dan leaned forward in his seat, drawn toward the openness. The sky felt higher here.

"This is it," Wyatt said, almost reverently. "The heart of the park, if you believe the brochures."

Dan didn't answer. He barely heard him.

Bison herds dotted the valley floor, slow-drifting shadows. Some moved in together, heads low to the ground. Others stood still as stones. From a distance, they looked like part of the terrain—alive, but anchored.

A bald eagle circled far overhead, banking slowly, its wings gliding through the turn.

Dan tracked it absently with his eyes, then let his gaze drift outward. A sloped clearing on the far side of the river caught his attention. Just above it, halfway up the treeline, something moved—deliberate, heavy.

A grizzly.

It was distant, a suggestion of weight and motion against the dark pines, but unmistakable. The way it moved—unhurried, self-contained—sent a current of something through him. Not fear. Not awe. Recognition.

He didn't point it out, sure Wyatt had already seen it, and not willing to break the moment with words.

Wyatt, watching the road. "They're waking up now," he said. "Bears. Otters. The works."

Dan nodded faintly.

The land was waking too.

They slowed near a pullout where a few vehicles had already parked, rental cars, a boxy camper van. A small group of people stood just beyond the shoulder; camera lenses pointed across the valley.

"Too far for a decent shot," Wyatt muttered.

As they eased past, Dan saw one man peel away from the group, stepping over the shallow drainage ditch and into the grass. Another followed. Their boots pressed into the wet ground, flattening fragile shoots not much taller than a finger. A woman crouched, holding her phone out in front of her like a shield.

"Jesus," Wyatt said, pulling the truck over. He let the engine idle. "I'll be back."

He stepped out and strode toward them, not fast, but with intent. Dan watched him gesture, polite but firm. Whatever he said carried weight. The tourists began shuffling back toward the pavement, eyes down. One of them spoke, gesturing with irritation, but Wyatt didn't take the bait.

Dan stayed in the truck.

The woman with the phone glanced up, and for a moment Dan thought she might lift it toward Wyatt.

But she didn't. She just turned, climbed into the camper, and shut the door.

Wyatt returned, boots muddy.

"Third time this week," he muttered, wiping his hands on his jeans. "People always need more."

Dan looked out across the valley. The grizzly had vanished.

They drove on in silence for a while, tires humming over the uneven pavement. A light breeze swept across the open flats.

Dan watched the land slide past—campers, tourists, crushed grass. Beneath it, the place was alive and ancient.

Protected. Picked over.

Still, something older pressed up through the soil.

The grizzly. The wolves.

They weren't a performance. Everything else was passing through.

Wyatt adjusted the rearview mirror. "You get used to the crowds," he said, as if catching Dan's train of thought. "Or you don't."

Dan didn't answer.

He didn't think he wanted to.

They pulled into a gravel turnout halfway between two river bends, the kind of spot most people missed. The Lamar shimmered below, shallow and wide, threading past banks of ice-burned grass and bleached driftwood.

Wyatt shut off the engine but didn't move right away. "Lunch?"

Dan glanced at his watch. "I didn't bring much."

"Me neither," Wyatt said, reaching behind the seat and tossing Dan a foil-wrapped packet. "Peanut butter and honey. My wife thinks I'm twelve."

Dan caught it, surprised. "Thanks."

They ate in silence for a while, leaning against opposite fenders. The sun had climbed high, softening the chill. Somewhere across the water, a kestrel called once, then went quiet.

Wyatt finally spoke. "So what made you leave Colorado?"

Dan took his time chewing. "I needed change, I guess. And space."

Wyatt nodded like he'd heard it before. "Space can be useful, if you let it."

Dan looked over at him. "What about you?"

"I came through with a fire crew one summer. Stuck around. It's pretty much all I know these days."

He scratched his chin, then gestured loosely at the landscape. "You think you're here to protect something. Then you think you're part of it. Then one day you realize it doesn't need you."

Dan waited, unsure if that was the end.

"The Park's got a heartbeat. But it doesn't beat for us. We just try not to screw it up too bad on our way through."

Dan nodded, comprehending something he instinctively already knew.

There was no bitterness in Wyatt's voice. Just knowledge worn smooth over time.

They finished their sandwiches in silence. Wyatt reached into the cab for a dented thermos and poured a bit into the cap. He held it out.

Dan took it. The coffee was lukewarm, bitter, and exactly right.

Wyatt leaned back and closed his eyes. "Bring that dog of yours out here tomorrow," he said. "We'll see what kind of trouble he can get into."

Dan blinked. "You sure?"

"Just don't let him lick tourists."

Dan smiled for the first time all day. "No promises."

Wyatt capped the thermos and gave it a small thump on the hood, like punctuation.

Dan caught Wyatt's gaze and said, "I watched a place go to hell in slow motion once."

Wyatt looked over but didn't speak.

"Just outside of Eagle. Used to be a stretch of scrubland, you'd see elk, mountain lions, a winter herd of mule deer. Then one year, the county okayed a cluster of luxury homes. 'Low impact,' they called it."

He shook his head, eyes on the distant line of cottonwoods.

"I remember watching a pair of badgers crossing the dirt road at dusk, right where the model home went up. The male paused at the road. I must've sat there ten minutes before I even put the truck in gear."

Wyatt didn't interrupt.

Dan shrugged. "Maybe it wasn't the last time. Maybe they found another way. But I didn't."

The breeze picked up again, lifting dry grass in small swells.

"I tried to report it," Dan added. "Document the impact—migration changes, predator scatter, all of it. But once people have their keys and lawn irrigation, no one wants to hear about animal patterns."

Wyatt made a quiet sound in his throat—not quite agreement and not quite surprise.

"Funny thing is," Dan said, "the animals still come. Just fewer. Warier. As if they're leaving a piece of themselves behind every season."

Wyatt reached for a toothpick from the console. "D'you ever get the feeling," he said, "that we're just tagging ghosts?"

Dan nodded. "Every year a little more."

They stood there a while longer, nothing more to prove or explain. Just two men on opposite ends of the same realization, watching the land do what it always had.

They got back in the truck and Wyatt started the engine and let it idle a moment before shifting into drive.

"What do you know about the park?" Wyatt asked, eyes on the horizon.

Dan glanced at him. "Only what most people know, I guess. It became a national park sometime in the late 1800s. First in the country."

Wyatt nodded. "1872. Ulysses S. Grant signed it in. That part's on the plaque at the north gate."

"Wasn't smooth sailing. No real management structure—just the U.S. Army patrolling out of Fort

Yellowstone. That started in the eighties. They did what they could, but it was rough. Poachers, squatters, cattlemen trying to graze wherever they wanted."

Dan turned toward him.

"After the Park Service took it over," Wyatt went on. "That's when they started building out the system. Roads and fire towers. Uniforms. Mission statements."

Dan watched the land blur—river bend, distant pine. The idea of "vision" felt wrong here. Like a word borrowed from somewhere else.

Wyatt gave a dry chuckle. "That's the story anyway. The white hats came in, cleaned it up, made it safe for visitors and viewfinders."

Dan didn't reply. He didn't need to.

No mention of who lived here before. No mention of who left.

Just the usual: founding dates, management shifts, fences and funding.

Wyatt slowed for a dip in the road, then looked sidelong at Dan. "You'll pick up the rest as you go. This place teaches you if you let it."

Dan nodded, but something in him had already begun turning over. A slow realization: that what he knew about this place was as curated as a trail map. The real story was harder to find. Maybe buried.

But not gone.

He turned to look out the window again as the road climbed gently into the next stretch of valley, wind tugging at the tops of the sagebrush.

Wyatt was quiet for a few miles, eyes on the road, a hand resting loose on the wheel. "Do you ever wonder how the hell this place survives four and a half million people a year?"

Dan blinked. The change in topic took him a second to catch. "I mean, yeah. It crossed my mind."

Wyatt grunted. "They come for the bears, the geysers, the selfies. Maybe a moose if they're lucky. But what they don't see is the plumbing. The backed-up vault toilets in July."

He angled the truck around a slow bend, where the Lamar River curved back toward them in a long silver ribbon.

"Staff housing's stretched thin. Rangers pulling double shifts. Volunteers doing the work of full-time people without pay or protections. But hey, the t-shirts are flying off the racks."

Dan didn't speak right away. The cynicism wasn't bitter—it felt more like fatigue worn down over years.

Wyatt went on. "Don't get me wrong. I've seen moments out here that could damn near crack your ribs open. Elk bugling across Swan Lake Flats in fog so thick you'd swear you were dreaming. Or a kid seeing his first bison up close and not breathing for a full minute."

He paused.

"But then someone tosses a diaper in a thermal vent. Or a drone hits a nesting eagle. And you think—Jesus, what're we doing?"

Dan nodded slowly. "Same pattern in Colorado. The access gets easier. People flood in. Everything gets—out of balance."

Wyatt glanced sideways. "Yeah, out of balance or, maybe broken."

They drove on for a while; both men lost in their own thoughts.

Then Dan asked, "What do you really need from a new ranger?"

Wyatt glanced over, one brow lifting just slightly.

"I mean, what's the actual mission? Out here. Besides handing out maps and keeping people from petting the bison."

Wyatt didn't answer right away.

"Keep your eyes open. Know your drainage. Show up when it matters."

He adjusted his grip on the wheel.

"And listen," he added. "Not just to people. Listen to the place. This park'll tell you when something's off, if you're paying attention. Most folks don't. They've already decided what they're seeing."

Dan nodded, slowly.

Wyatt looked out at the valley one last time before the trees began to close in again.

"We don't need heroes," he said. "We need someone who won't look away when the job gets ugly. Who gives a damn even when no one's watching."

The words weren't sentimental. They were worn and plain and spoken in truth.

The road rose gently ahead. The outline of Mammoth shimmered in the distance.

Behind them, Lamar stretched out—vast, wild, and waiting.

SIXTEEN

DAN WAS TIGHTENING THE STRAPS on the bear-proof food locker behind housing when his phone rang. The screen lit with a number he didn't recognize.

He hesitated, then answered.

"Nowak," came the familiar voice. "How's the wolf boy doing?"

Dan smiled despite himself. "Hey, Tom."

"Didn't think you'd pick up," Tom said. "I thought maybe you'd gone full radio silence up there."

"Almost," Dan said. "Service is spotty unless I'm standing on the propane tank."

Tom laughed. "Figures. Listen, I'm down in Jackson for a couple days. Mountain Law Enforcement conference. Mostly suits and slide decks, but they feed us well. Figured I'd see if you wanted to meet up."

Dan scratched at the back of his neck. The sun was sharp today, but snowmelt still ran in veins across the gravel lot. He had a couple of days off. Nothing planned.

"How long are you here?"

"Just until Friday. I'm buying dinner tonight if you drive down."

Dan hesitated. Jackson was close, but not casual-close. A couple hours over the pass. And he'd only just started to find his footing in the park—still learning who to nod at and who to avoid, still figuring out which voices on the radio to trust.

But he couldn't find a good reason to say no.

"Yeah," he said finally. "I could make that work."

"Good man," Tom said. "I'll text you the place. Nothing fancy. Bring that dog of yours if you want."

Dan glanced over at the housing unit, where Shankley lay flopped in the shadow of the stairs.

"Maybe."

Tom paused. "How are you doing?"

Dan considered the question.

"Getting there," he said.

"All right," Tom replied. "See you tonight, wolf boy."

Dan looked out toward the ridgeline, where a pale line of clouds was forming above the trees. He didn't feel like driving. But maybe that was the point.

Dan eased the truck into Jackson just past four. The town was bustling. Crosswalk signs blinked. Storefront flags flapped. A line of tourists in fleece and trail runners hung around outside an ice cream shop, despite the chill still hanging in the air.

It reminded him of parts of Colorado, but with antler arches and art galleries that leaned harder into rustic than refined.

He passed a fly shop with three different models of rod displayed in the front window, each with hand-lettered price tags that could cover a week's pay. Next door, a gallery offered "Fine Wildlife Bronzework."

The Tetons loomed behind it all—sharp-edged, snow-capped, impossible to ignore. They framed the town, their wildness the backdrop to a storefront facade.

Dan caught a green light and rolled through the town square. The shops blurred into real estate offices and outfitters. Even the gas stations had wood paneling and polished river rock along the base.

He didn't mind it. But everything felt like it had been tuned a little too tight.

At a stop sign, a lifted SUV rolled by, its rear window covered with brand decals—gear companies, guide services, a brewery. He noticed the small sticker tucked in the corner: KEEP JACKSON WILD.

Dan raised an eyebrow.

He turned left toward the lodge Tom had texted him earlier. Cedar siding, wide balconies, a row of spotless full-size SUVs out front. A woman in a puffy vest carried a tiny dog past the valet stand, chatting on her phone.

Dan pulled into a side space and killed the engine.

For a long moment, he just sat there, hands resting on the wheel. Shankley stirred beside him and let out a sigh.

Dan reached over and gave him a scratch behind the ears. "It's only one night."

He stepped out, stretched, and looked up at the mountains—unmoving and unimpressed.

Dan stepped through the automatic doors, a rush of warm air brushing against his face. A fireplace crackled off to the left, flames dancing behind glass. Above it hung a framed black-and-white photo of a cowboy wrangling cattle, the kind of image that felt less like history and more like decor.

He approached the front desk, where a young man in a pressed vest looked up from a tablet.

"Evening," Dan said. "I'm looking for a guest—Tom Delaney."

The clerk's smile flicked on like a switch. "Certainly, sir. One moment." His fingers tapped quickly across the screen. "Yes, Mr. Delaney is staying with us. I can call for you?"

Dan nodded. "Please."

The clerk picked up the phone, dialed with an effortless rhythm. "Mr. Delaney? I have a gentleman here at the front desk. Of course. I'll let him know."

He hung up and smiled again. "You're expected. Room 208. Elevator's just around the corner to your left."

Dan thanked him and turned toward the elevator. The lobby was quiet. An older couple sipped wine near the fireplace, murmuring about snowpack and river levels. A little girl in hiking boots carried a stuffed fox under one arm, trailing a tired-looking father with a North Face duffel.

He pressed the elevator button. The light blinked. Somewhere above, machinery stirred.

Shankley had stayed curled in the truck, windows cracked, bed in the back. He felt a tug in his gut—like he should've brought him in, even if he knew it wasn't allowed.

The elevator opened with a chime.

Dan stepped inside and watched the door close.

The second-story hallway was lined with photographs of sepia-toned bison, snow-laced peaks, a lone fly fisherman casting into a mirror-still river. The carpet was too soft under Dan's boots. Every step felt padded and muffled, like walking through someone else's version of the West.

He found room 208 near the end of the hall.

Raised his hand.

For a moment, he just stood there.

Something about the door felt heavier than it should. Not physically—just in the way it separated this quiet, curated lodge from everything he'd left behind—Colorado, the old job, the rhythms he'd come to depend on.

Tom was a part of all that. Dan wasn't sure if he wanted it back.

He rubbed his thumb against his knuckles. Then knocked.

The door opened almost instantly.

"About time," Tom said, grinning.

He looked the same—laugh lines crinkled, grounded as ever. Plaid shirt with the sleeves rolled.

Dan felt the tension slide off his shoulders.

"Hey," he said, and stepped inside.

Tom clapped him on the back as he passed. "Still carrying that distant look. Are you sleeping at all?"

"Some," Dan said. "Are you still talking too much?"

Tom laughed. "Only when I'm trying to be annoying."

The room was neat, practical—two beds, a table, and a pair of boots kicked half-under the chair. Tom's gear bag was slouched open in the corner, topped with a folder marked MLEN – Agenda.

Dan nodded toward it. "Learning how to write more citations?"

"Hell no," Tom said. "Mostly meetings about grant funding and body cams. One guy gave a whole presentation on improved zip-tie ergonomics."

Dan raised an eyebrow.

Tom shrugged. "We live in the future now, brother."

He handed Dan a bottle of water from the fridge. "Dinner's in an hour. But sit. Catch me up."

Dan sank into the chair by the window, the view showing nothing but a parking lot and the lower hem of the Tetons. He took a sip of water and remembered that Tom had been a friend, and maybe he still was.

* * *

They walked to dinner under sky the color of hammered tin. Tom moved with easy familiarity, pointing out shops and bad restaurant memories as they passed.

"If you ever want the driest elk burger of your life, that place back there's your answer," he said, thumbing toward a dim-lit grill with antlers over the door. "Swear it was made from a retired mount."

Dan let the words roll past. He wasn't quite up for Tom's banter, but his friend didn't seem to mind carrying the conversation.

The town was busy but not frantic—just enough motion to keep the sidewalks pulsing. Streetlamps flicked on as they walked, catching the shimmer of water pooling in curbside cracks.

The place Tom had picked was one of those modern-rustic joints—reclaimed wood walls, Edison bulbs over the bar, and a soft glow spilling from the open kitchen in the back. It smelled like grilled meat and charred rosemary.

A host in a denim apron led them to a small table near the front window. Most of the other tables were filled with conference types—men and women in fitted fleece vests and clean hiking boots, half-talking shop and half talking real estate.

Tom picked up the beer list and raised an eyebrow. "You want something with a name like 'Wild Basin Burial' or whatever's cold?"

Dan smirked. "Surprise me."

They ordered burgers and two local drafts that arrived in frosted pint glasses, both darker than expected.

Tom clinked his glass against Dan's. "To surviving the last year and still holding on, and without committing a felony."

Dan took a sip. "Jury's still out."

Tom leaned back in his chair, surveying the room. "Everyone here looks like they're two paychecks away from founding a wilderness retreat."

Dan watched a couple at the next table—polished gear, practiced laughs. She was showing him something on her phone. He nodded without really looking.

"D'you ever think it's all just a little too clean?" Dan asked.

Tom shrugged. "It's Jackson."

Dan didn't say more. But something in him folded back again. The town moved around them—a well-oiled machine, humming with money, progress, and curated nature.

And yet, across the Tetons, the park waited.

Tom nudged his glass forward. "You're doing better than you think."

Dan looked up. "I don't know about that."

Tom smiled, not unkindly. "I've known you long enough to spot the difference between tired and lost."

Dan took another drink.

Didn't agree.

Didn't argue.

Let it sit there, between them, like the mountains behind the window.

Their plates arrived, the burgers piled high, fries stacked vertical in a paper funnel. Dan was halfway through when he set it down and wiped his hands on the cloth napkin, eyes drifting toward the window again.

Tom let the silence sit. He'd always been good at that—holding a space without needing to fill it.

"I didn't leave Colorado because of the job," Dan asserted finally.

Tom glanced up. Waited.

“I left because I stopped feeling anything. Like, the animals were still there. The calls came in. But I’d be out in the field and it was just... empty. Like I was running through the motions when I should have been doing more.”

Tom nodded, slowly.

Dan went on. “This park’s different. It’s not clean. Not polished. It doesn’t care what you want from it. And the wildlife... it’s more. Even though it’s all been managed, tracked, shaped by people—there’s still this sense, out in certain parts, of what came before. Like you’re catching the edge of a time when herds moved untouched. When nothing flinched at the sound of a motor.”

He picked up his beer, studied the foam clinging to the glass. “It’s hard to explain.”

Tom leaned back, letting that hang.

“I get that,” he said. “A place like that doesn’t lie to you. If something dies, it rots. If something survives, it does it out loud.”

Dan smiled faintly. “That’s pretty much it.”

Tom set down his glass. “I figured something had cracked. Back in the fall. You were quieter. Less... I don’t know. Less tethered.”

Dan nodded. “Yeah. And I didn’t want to pretend otherwise anymore. I just didn’t know what came after.”

“You still don’t,” Tom said, not unkindly. “But you’re closer.”

They both sat with that for a moment.

Outside, the last of the daylight faded. A row of headlights blinked down the street, trailing past boutique shopfronts and a rack of rental bikes nobody was touching in the cold.

Tom looked at Dan. "You gonna stick with it?"

Dan thought about that. "I think the park's got more to teach me."

Tom smiled. "That's probably the best reason to stay anywhere."

They clinked glasses again, no toast this time. Just a small gesture of recognition. Of a bond holding true across miles and time.

Tom leaned back, thumb tracing the edge of his glass. "Kira heard from Allison, by the way. Just in passing."

Dan looked up, surprised.

"She's good," Tom said. "Settled in Boulder. Sounds like the shop's giving her more responsibility. Maybe too much."

Dan nodded slowly. "Good," he said. And he meant it.

There was a pause. Not awkward—just... careful.

"I wasn't sure," Dan added. "How things landed. I didn't exactly make it easy."

Tom didn't argue. Didn't excuse it, either. Just said, "No one comes out of something like that clean."

Dan gave a faint smile. "Yeah."

But the relief was there. A knot in his chest he'd avoided starting to loosen.

They stepped out into the cold. The streetlights cast long shadows across the sidewalks now, and the Tetons were just hidden behind the dark.

Tom tilted his head toward the square. "One more?"

Dan gave him a look. "You serious?"

Tom grinned. "Million Dollar Cowboy Bar. It's a rite of passage."

Dan hesitated.

Tom clapped him on the shoulder. "You already crossed the border. Might as well get the stamp. You can stay the night; there's an extra bed."

When they finally got back to the lodge, it was nearly midnight, the lobby empty except for a sleepy-eyed desk clerk half-watching the weather on mute.

Tom glanced over at Dan as they approached the door. "So—are we doing this?"

Dan sighed. "It's your hotel."

Tom grinned. "And your dog."

Shankley perked up in the back seat as Dan cracked the truck door. He opened the door wider and gave a low whistle. "Stay close," he murmured.

The dog jumped down with enthusiasm and absolutely no sense of stealth, nuzzling Tom like he was a long-lost friend.

Tom winced. "Ninja."

They crept toward the side entrance like teenagers sneaking in after curfew—Tom in the lead, Dan towing a well-meaning mutt trying to sniff every parked tire along the way.

At the door, Dan fumbled the keycard. It beeped red.

Tom hissed, "You had one job."

Dan tried again. Green.

They slipped inside, nodding curtly to a potted plant like it was a witness.

In the hallway, a housekeeper's cart sat abandoned near the elevator. Tom paused, looked at the unattended stack of towels, then looked at Dan.

Dan shook his head. "No."

"Just saying," Tom whispered, "in case the dog wants a disguise."

Dan gave him a look.

The elevator opened with a soft chime. A man stepped out and barely glanced at them—just two guys with a happy-looking dog.

Inside the room, Shankley did a slow circuit, sniffed the corner, and flopped down with a grunt like he'd been personally carrying the emotional weight of the evening.

Tom pulled off his boots. "See? Seamless operation."

Dan collapsed onto the edge of the bed. "I think we committed three violations of lodge policy."

Tom opened the minibar and held up a tiny bottle. "Make it four?"

Dan managed a tired laugh. "You're a terrible cop."

Tom passed him the bottle anyway. "Yeah. But you're not going back to that truck, and I'm not letting you spend the night pretending you're fine."

Dan didn't answer right away. Just opened the bottle and tipped it back.

Outside, the wind moved softly against the window. Inside, a dog snored, and two men who'd seen too much and said too little for too long, sat in the kind of silence that didn't need fixing.

SEVENTEEN

RITA DIDN'T LOOK UP when they walked in. She was flipping through a thin manila folder, dog-eared at the edges, a list of crossed out recipients on the cover.

"How do you feel about kids?" she asked, still scanning a page.

Wyatt made a low groaning sound in his throat. Dan stayed quiet.

Rita glanced up. "That's what I thought."

She closed the folder and set it down. "Principal Wallace up at Gardiner sent a request. He wants someone from Wildlife to talk to the eighth grade."

Rita glanced from one ranger to another.

"One of their teachers is a fireball—his words, not mine. They like to expand the syllabus. The principal wants this one to stay on track. Wildlife only. No soapboxes. No Bigfoot theories."

Wyatt raised an eyebrow. "You're thinking of me?"

"Absolutely not," Rita said, dry. "Last time you did a school visit, I got a call from a fifth grader's mom. The kid had nightmares for a week."

Wyatt grinned. "Nature's rough."

"Exactly why you're not going," she said, and then turned to Dan. "Congratulations. You win the short straw."

Dan leaned against the doorframe, arms crossed. "Eighth grade?"

"Gardiner K–12. Tomorrow morning. You'll be speaking in the science wing, first period. Mr. Wallace seemed polite enough, but between the lines, I think he's worried his eighth-grade teacher is trying to radicalize the children."

"Radicalize how?"

"She likes to talk about the park's full history. Eleven thousand years' worth. He wants a clean wildlife talk. Moose, bears, migration patterns. Nothing that'll show up in a superintendent memo."

Wyatt muttered, "Sounds like a setup."

Rita gave him a look. "It's a favor. We do favors to keep people happy."

Dan said nothing, but he felt a twinge of interest. Maybe, not in the school or the kids, but in the idea that someone in that building might actually want to talk about the parts of Yellowstone that didn't make it onto the plaques.

* * *

Leona Windreed's classroom smelled like whiteboard markers. A laminated poster of Yellowstone's wildlife stretched along one wall, faded at the edges. The back bulletin board housed student projects with construction paper borders fluttered under a ceiling vent. Some kind of geology unit, judging by the cut-out layers of earth and plastic gemstone stickers.

Dan stood near the door, out of the way but visible. He could see the teacher was already inside, collecting a stray worksheet from a desk, tapping it twice to square the corners before sliding it into a folder. She was younger than he'd expected—not by age, but in energy. Her presence seemed to fill the room.

She turned toward the class with a practiced ease. "Alright, folks," she said, raising her voice just slightly over the rustling of backpacks. "Eyes up here. Phones away. No exceptions, Devin."

A few choruses of yes Ms. Windreed went around, and a boy in the back pocketed something without looking up.

"We've got a guest this morning from the Wildlife Service." She glanced at Dan briefly, then back to the room. "His name is Dan Nowak. That's *No-wak*, not *No-vack*, so let's make sure to get it right."

Dan gave a short nod but didn't smile.

She continued, "Mr. Nowak is here to talk about Yellowstone's wildlife from a management perspective—which is not the same as a YouTube video or a survival show. This is boots-on-the-ground knowledge, so I expect decent questions and better listening."

Her tone had altered—still firm, still engaging, but with a thin thread of formality that hadn't been there a moment ago.

Dan noticed it. He'd been in classrooms before. Some teachers made space for him; others kept their distance. This one—he couldn't tell yet.

Leona didn't sit. She moved to the edge of the room, one hip against a low cabinet, arms folded, watching—not Dan, but the students.

They were sizing him up the way kids do. Eighth graders with a sixth sense for authenticity. If he was going to bluff or bore, they'd tune him out before he finished his second sentence.

Dan stood at the front with the awkward posture of someone used to open air, not fluorescent light. He wore a plain forest service fleece with no badge. That earned him a point in Leona's mental tally.

He started to talk.

He didn't have any notes or a slideshow. Just his voice, steady and unhurried. A ranger's voice—not in tone, but in restraint. Everything he said had been sifted first and stripped of excess.

She glanced toward Star, who had stopped chewing her pen and was now fully still. There it was. That subtle lean of attention. A ripple.

Dan asked a question about vision, asking if they'd ever looked through a magnifying glass, or tried on a pair of reading glasses. A few nodded. One or two muttered examples. Dan let them. He didn't jump to regain control.

Then he said something that made Leona tilt her head.

"That's how an animal might feel if it had to see the world the way we do. They see *some* things in clear focus while other things are just not important."

He didn't explain it further. Letting it take root.

Leona narrowed her eyes slightly. That wasn't a line from the wildlife management handbook. That was something else—something lived.

She looked at him again, really looked this time.

There was nothing performative in his stance. But there was weight. Like the words cost him something. Like he'd come by them the long way.

Her arms uncrossed slowly. She made a small note in her head, unrelated to the curriculum. She'd talk to him after.

Not because he was a ranger. But because something about the way he said that—that small, quiet shift in the room—told her he wasn't just here to give a talk.

Dan kept it simple.

He spoke of elk migration, wolf tracking collars, how bison moved differently in winter depending on wind direction. He touched on bear hibernation; how young males roamed further and took risks the older ones avoided. He didn't bring up management policies or the tension behind predator balance.

Still, he found a rhythm. The students weren't restless and a few took notes. Most listened in that soft, glazed way—not bored, just drifting slightly. Dan was fine with that.

When he opened it up for questions, a few hands went up hesitantly.

David, a lanky kid in a Yellowstone hoodie asked, "Have you ever been chased by anything?"

A ripple of laughter passed through the room.

Dan smiled, just a little. "Once or twice. Usually it's not personal."

He didn't make a joke out of it, didn't laugh with them or at them. Just answered flatly, honestly and that seemed to land.

Star raised her hand.

She'd been quiet the whole time, sharp-eyed. A kid who saw through things. Leona watched her closely.

Star didn't wait for Dan to call on her.

"If animals see differently," she said, "do you think they also feel things differently? Like... not just fear or hunger. But... I don't know. The world. What things are important?"

The room went still.

Dan didn't speak right away.

He looked at her. Not like a teacher, not like a ranger. Just looked.

And then he said, "Yeah. I do."

He let out a slow breath, almost imperceptible.

"When I talk about sight," he said, "I don't just mean what they see, I mean how they're *in* what they see. There's no gap. A crow doesn't fly above the world; it *belongs* to it. It's not just looking for a meal. It's mapping scent, sound, the currents in the air. All at once."

He paused.

"I don't think it's about instincts or survival. Not entirely. I think... there's a kind of knowing that doesn't translate. Not into words. Not into what we'd call feelings either. But it's there. You can feel it if you're quiet enough."

Leona's arms folded again, but this time it wasn't distance but focus.

Dan hadn't rehearsed that. He spoke like someone who'd been there.

And now the whole class was quiet. Even David.

No one spoke right away.

Even the kids who usually had something snarky at the ready were quiet—caught between the sense that something had just been said, and not knowing exactly what it was.

Star sat back in her chair, not triumphant, just thoughtful. Like she'd expected the answer, or maybe part of it had already lived in her, waiting for someone else to say it aloud.

Leona didn't move. She wasn't watching the students anymore. She was watching Dan.

He seemed almost surprised by his own words. Not embarrassed, not shaken, but like he hadn't meant to open the door that far.

One of the ceiling lights buzzed faintly.

Outside, a black bird passed by the window, a single wingbeat visible before it disappeared beyond the frame.

Dan blinked. Cleared his throat.

"That's probably more philosophical than you were looking for," he said, with a dry edge meant to signal an ending.

But no one laughed. No one broke the silence.

Leona stepped forward and tapped the windowsill with her fingers—three quick knocks.

"Alright," she said, her voice easy but firm. "That's time."

There was a shuffling of chairs and a few deep exhales.

Dan stepped back, letting the class settle, letting the class routine return. He didn't look at Star again. But she looked at him.

So did Leona.

And in both their eyes, there wasn't just curiosity. There was recognition.

The last of the students filed out, footsteps echoing down the hall. Star gave Dan a glance on her way through the door—not a smile exactly, more a trace of connection.

Dan turned to gather himself, half-reaching for the water bottle he hadn't touched. He didn't notice the man in the doorway until he spoke.

"Well done," the man said. "Not always easy keeping that group engaged, but they looked sharp and attentive."

Dan straightened a little. The man wore a sport coat over a checkered shirt, the kind of tie that suggested he only wore one when someone might be looking.

"Principal Wallace," he said, extending a hand. "Thanks for coming up from Mammoth."

Dan shook it. "Dan Nowak."

Wallace's handshake was dry and quick. "I appreciate you making the time. We like to keep things fresh for the eighth-graders. I think you gave them a lot to think about."

Dan nodded once, unsure how to respond. He sensed there was more coming.

Wallace turned toward Leona. "Ms. Windreed, how would you say the class responded?"

Leona's expression didn't shift. She knew the rhythm of this dance.

"They listened," she said evenly. "They asked good questions. I think they picked up more than they usually do."

"Mmhmm." Wallace smiled in that practiced way of administrators who already knew the answer they were looking for. "You wouldn't say there were tangents or disruptions?"

Leona's smile was thinner. "Not from me."

Dan glanced between them. It wasn't hostile but careful. Something old, and ongoing.

"Well," Wallace said, clapping his hands together once, softly, "I'll let you get back to it. Mr. Nowak, thank you again for your time. Always good to have a real-world voice in the room."

Dan gave a small nod. "Thanks for having me."

Wallace offered another short smile, then disappeared into the hallway with the smooth efficiency of someone who preferred to be seen leaving than standing still.

As his footsteps faded, Leona exhaled just slightly.

"That," she said under her breath, "was Mr. Wallace checking my leash."

Dan raised an eyebrow. He already understood more than she'd said.

The door clicked shut behind Wallace.

Leona stayed where she was, arms still loosely folded, gaze fixed on the empty desks like something was still unfolding in the air.

Dan looked at her then. Not just in the way you look at someone who's spoken, but like a second pass. A truer one.

She was clearly Native, he didn't know from where and he didn't assume, but it was there in the set of her cheekbones, the straight fall of her dark hair pulled back loosely. There was pride in her posture, not arrogance. She wasn't trying to impress anyone and she didn't need to.

And she didn't seem hard. He'd met people who taught with edge, sharpness, like they were proving something, but Leona wasn't that. Her presence felt steadier. Intentional. As if every step she took in that classroom, every word had been chosen.

He could see now why she went her own way with lessons.

There was something in her—something that regarded boundaries not as limits, but as invitations.

Dan wasn't sure if that unsettled him or pulled him closer.

She looked over and caught his eye.

"You didn't give them the usual ranger talk," she said.

He shrugged, a small thing. "Didn't feel right."

Leona studied him for a moment longer, then nodded once, like that confirmed something she'd already suspected.

She stepped away from the cabinet and moved toward the door, her tone easy again.

"I'll walk you out."

Dan followed, the hallway mostly empty now, just a few younger kids herding themselves toward lunch or recess. Their footsteps echoed against the cinder block walls. A display case held state science fair ribbons and a dusty model of a geyser mid-eruption.

They moved in a companionable silence until they reached the front vestibule. Through the double doors, the sky had gone soft with thin clouds, and the wind was carrying a trace of sage from somewhere further down the valley.

Leona paused with her hand on the door.

"I take the long way through the park sometimes," she said. "During the off-hours to dodge the tourists and really take my time."

Dan nodded, unsure if she was just making conversation.

"There are over 1,800 archaeological sites in the park," she went on. "That's just what's been recorded. Most people don't know that."

He glanced over. "I didn't."

Leona looked out toward the road, then back at him.

"If you're ever interested... I don't mind company."

She didn't wait for a response. Just pushed the door open and held it with one hand, letting the spring-loaded hinge creak slightly.

Dan stepped through. The cold hit him in the chest—high mountain chill, even in spring.

He turned back to thank her, but she was already moving, heading down the concrete steps like she had somewhere to be.

She'd left a quiet invitation, laid down and waiting to be picked up.

Dan sat in the driver's seat, the engine off, the faint creak of the frame as the wind slid around the parked body of the truck.

He hadn't put his hands on the wheel yet. Just sat there, looking out through the windshield at the school's flagpole, the lot half full, the low line of the mountains beyond.

Eighteen hundred archaeological sites. He hadn't known that. He probably should have, working where he did. But he hadn't thought to ask—not about what had come before.

And the way she moved in a quiet self-assured way, but in that unshakable way people have when they know where they come from.

Dan shifted in his seat. That thing he'd said about the crow, it had come out without warning. Not scripted, not vetted. He didn't regret it, exactly, but it had cracked something open. And she'd seen it.

Not judged it, or questioned it.

Just—seen it.

He looked out toward the ridge. Somewhere beyond that was the park boundary. Miles of forest and river, stone and wind. And beneath all of that—something old.

EIGHTEEN

DAN HEARD THE TRUCK before he saw it—a familiar sound. It wound up the hill toward the cluster of employee housing near the maintenance compound.

He stepped off the low porch as Leona pulled up.

A charcoal-grey Toyota Tacoma. Two years newer than his. Same lift, similar off-road tires. He couldn't help the small grin that pulled at the corner of his mouth.

Leona rolled down the passenger window. "Nice driveway," she said, glancing at the cracked pavement.

Dan opened the door and slid in. The cab was tidy and didn't smell of wet dog, a definite upgrade from his own truck.

"Tacoma," he said, settling in. "Had mine since college, could never seem to let it go."

He tapped the dash lightly. "Mine's green. A little more—patina."

She nodded.

"I did a lot of walking in college but finally managed to scrape enough together for a used one. I'll try not to hold it against you."

He glanced over. She wasn't smiling, exactly, but there was a spark. Dry, understated, easy.

She shifted into reverse, checked her mirror, and backed out onto the narrow road that would take them toward the north entrance and into the wider sweep of the park.

They drove in silence for a while. Not awkward, just quiet.

Dan looked out the window at the rising light over the ridgeline. The low sun had touched the upper flanks of the hills, green grass bright from the new growth of spring.

"Where are we going?" he asked eventually.

Leona kept her eyes on the road. "Nowhere people go on purpose."

They took a turn past the upper service yard and followed the winding road that dropped them toward the park entrance. Light filtered in through the windshield, catching dust on the dash.

Dan cleared his throat lightly. "You know, I wasn't sure this was going to happen."

Leona glanced at him, one hand on the wheel. "What do you mean?"

"I wasn't sure how to contact you."

She said nothing, just waited.

"I told the school I thought I left something behind. A water bottle or—maybe a notebook. Got the vice-principal—Walsh, I think?"

Leona snorted softly. "Justine! You should have just asked her for my number."

He shifted in the seat, watching the road rise and fall ahead of them.

"I said if Ms. Windrush found anything, she could give me a call."

"Ms. Windreed."

He looked over. "Right. Windreed."

She smiled now, just barely. "You left a fake water bottle and got my name wrong. That's impressive."

Dan gave a small shrug. "Well, I didn't want to go through Wallace. Figured I'd screw it up if I tried to make it official."

They lapsed into an easy silence.

Outside the window the land was opening up. Sage and open meadows, the hills rolling broad and bare before the forest picked up again.

They passed through the Roosevelt Arch and angled south. Leona drove with one hand on the wheel, steady and relaxed. The cab filled with the rhythm of tires on pavement and the faint hiss of wind through the cracked passenger window.

Dan glanced out at the open land, the early green starting to wake in patches across the hills.

Leona spoke without preamble. "Most people think the park started in 1872."

Dan nodded, he'd thought that too.

She continued, "Well that's what the signs say. What every school tour guide and plaque tries to teach. But they're off by a few zeros."

He looked over at her.

"There's evidence of human presence in this basin going back more than eleven thousand years," she said. "Obsidian tools and fire pits. Campsites buried in sediment."

Dan let that sink in.

"Do you teach that?" he asked.

"I try."

Dan nodded. "And the school's not on board."

"Wallace isn't a bad guy. Just—institutional. He wants balance, which usually means erasure with a smile." Her voice wasn't bitter. Just practiced. "He says I can talk about Native history if I keep it 'cultural' and don't imply it's ongoing."

Dan didn't know what to say to that.

Leona adjusted her grip on the wheel. "Do you ever notice the way people talk about nature like it's a place you visit?"

He gave a small breath of agreement. "Like it starts at the trailhead."

"Exactly." She pointed toward a cluster of dark pines cresting a ridge. "But this place, Yellowstone, didn't wait for us to show up and name it. People lived here. Left things. Prayed, buried, healed. For millennia."

Dan looked out at the land again, and he could see what she meant.

"You said there were eighteen hundred archaeological sites," he said.

She nodded. "That's just what's been recorded. Every time the park does a construction project, they trip over something. Usually they don't say much about it. Might complicate the story."

They drove on, past shallow draws and scattered cottonwood. A golden eagle circled above, ever wider circles as it searched for prey.

Dan watched it for a moment.

"I thought I was starting to understand this place," he said. "I get how the animals have been part of it forever, but I suppose our focus is always the last hundred years or less."

Leona didn't respond right away.

"That's most people."

She slowed slightly for a curve, tires hugging the inside edge where the road met a sheer slope of scree and scrub.

"The tourists come here for the big stuff," she said. "Geysers. Wolves. Peaks. Something that makes them feel small. But they don't want to feel like they don't matter, insignificant. Part of something so old they don't even get to have a name in the story."

A line of elk came into view off the shoulder—half a dozen cows moving single file through the brush, ears flicking toward the road but not spooked. Leona waited and let them pass without a word.

When the elk were gone, Leona picked up speed again, easy on the gas. Her gaze stayed fixed on the road, but her voice had softened slightly.

"I don't need people to believe anything," she said. "Not about spirits or ancestors or sacred ground. I just want them to stop pretending the past isn't still breathing."

Dan looked over at her.

And for the first time since she'd picked him up, he felt like he was being taken somewhere, somewhere he wouldn't have found on his own.

They drove in silence for a few more miles, the land growing wider, flatter. Leona flicked her turn signal and pulled off into a narrow turnout, a break in the guardrail, a place you only stopped if you knew.

She put the truck in park and killed the engine.

Dan followed her gaze.

Below them, in a broad meadow, a herd of bison moved slowly through the grass. Thirty or forty animals, grazing and ambling in loose formation. Calves stayed close to mothers while a few bulls stood apart, half-sentry and half-indifferent.

Dan leaned forward against the dash.

The herd was a few hundred yards out, but they felt closer.

One of the older bulls turned its massive head and looked toward them, then went back to feeding.

"This is one of the original herds," Leona said eventually. "Their bloodlines go back further than the park."

Dan didn't respond. He didn't need to. The sight of the herd had calmed him. Still, he felt like something was coming. A history he hadn't been taught.

But for now, he just watched the bison move—slow, deliberate, unbothered by the road or the humans watching from above.

Leona rested her arms on the steering wheel, eyes still on the herd.

"I teach this to my eighth graders in pieces," she said. "I clean it up, make it measured. Then it's palatable enough to make it past Wallace and the history standards."

Dan glanced at her, but she didn't look over.

"But with you, I don't have to pretend it was a mistake."

She nodded toward the bison below.

"Before European settlement, there were somewhere between thirty and sixty million of them on the continent. Sixty million," she said again, quieter this time. "They roamed from northern Canada to the Gulf of Mexico. They moved in herds so massive it could take hours for one to pass."

She took a steadying breath.

"And then, in less than fifty years, they were nearly gone. Not by accident. Not by overhunting. Not because someone needed meat or hides. It was policy. A tool."

Dan didn't move. The silence between them had grown heavier, but not oppressive.

"They were wiped out to starve Native people. To cut supply lines. To force relocation. General Sheridan said it, 'Let them kill, skin and sell until the buffalo is exterminated...'" She trailed off for a moment. "It was cheaper than war."

The herd below continued to move, a few calves trotting to keep pace as the adults meandered toward the river's bend.

Leona's voice didn't tremble, but there was something tight beneath it.

"I can't say it like that in the classroom. I have to call it an 'impact of expansion.' I have to say the word 'decline' like it just... happened. Like the bison just walked off a cliff."

Dan looked down at the herd. The animals looked ancient even from here; coarse, dark, and earthen.

"Was it just this herd that survived?" he asked.

"A few pockets. This one's the only continuous wild population in the lower forty-eight. But it was close. Real close."

She finally turned to him.

"They wanted the people gone, so they made the land empty first. And now it's a park."

His stomach tightened and his fist clenched as he worked through her words.

"I didn't know that." he said finally.

He hated how small that sounded. How incomplete.

Leona didn't look at him, letting the moment hang.

Dan leaned forward, forearms on his knees, eyes fixed on the bison.

"I knew the population collapsed. Everyone knows that part. But I didn't know..." He shook his head once. "I didn't know it was on purpose."

"Feels like we wrote a story about the land," he said quietly, "a story that is full of holes."

Leona let out a slow breath through her nose. Not a laugh or agreement, but recognition.

"That's the curriculum," she said.

They sat there another moment. Two people in a parked truck above a herd of survivors.

Leona started the engine again, the sound of the Tacoma coughing to life breaking the spell.

They turned back onto the road and continued south, following the gentle curve of the river in the distance. The valley opened and narrowed again. Leona pointed with her chin as they passed a narrow pullout.

"That's where they found the stone blades last summer. Blades with obsidian points, shaped by heat, and still sharp."

Dan looked, but there was nothing to see—just grass, a few weather-worn rocks, a cottonwood snag leaning toward the river. You'd never know what lay beneath it unless you were looking.

"Some of the stone was from hundreds of miles away," she added. "Trade routes ran through here long before it was a park."

Dan nodded, not because he fully grasped it, but because it deserved a nod.

They drove on. The road dropped slightly, following the slope of the terrain. The trees thickened, then broke again, revealing a stretch of the river just off to the right—clear, wide and slow-moving in parts, with a few gentle riffles curling around exposed stone.

Leona eased off the pavement onto a dirt track that led down toward the bank. The truck rocked slightly as they made the rocky descent.

"This is one of my favorite spots," she said, voice soft now. "Nobody comes this far off trail unless they know it."

She pulled to a stop beneath a stand of cottonwoods. A few birds scattered from the branches overhead. The river lay just beyond, glinting silver and pale blue in the afternoon light.

Dan opened the door slowly and stepped out. The air was cooler here, clean and full of the scent of water, bark, and a trace of moss. He felt it hit him low in the chest, like something drawing him forward without words.

He didn't say anything. Just walked to the edge of the bank and crouched near the rocks, hands loose at his sides.

Leona watched him for a moment.

And then, just beyond where the water slid around a cluster of stone, something dark and sinuous moved—sleek, low, and fast.

An otter.

It broke the surface with ease, twisting once in the current before disappearing again beneath it.

Dan didn't move.

His breathing slowed.

And Leona, still standing beside the truck, narrowed her eyes.

Dan felt something in him realigning.

Not like zoning out. Not like distraction or fatigue.

It was quieter than that. Deeper.

Leona took a slow step forward.

The otter surfaced again, just briefly, head slick, whiskers glinting, a flash of motion too quick to anchor.

Then it vanished beneath the waterline with nothing but a ripple left behind.

Dan stayed crouched, unmoving. His eyes were open, but something had turned inward. Like the world had narrowed and widened at the same time.

Leona stood a few feet behind, watching.

She'd seen people check out before—kids in class, overwhelmed parents, even Wallace when she pushed too far. There was a blankness to it, a drifting.

But this wasn't that.

This wasn't absence. It was presence of a different kind.

She stepped forward, slowly, careful not to crowd him.

"People think stillness means nothing's happening," she said, her voice barely more than a breath. "But sometimes it's the only way something *can* happen."

Dan didn't answer. He barely blinked.

Leona studied his posture—the looseness of it, the lack of defense. It wasn't vulnerability in the usual sense. It was... openness. Like a doorway slightly ajar.

"I've seen kids in trance," she said carefully. "Ceremony. Story. Grief."

She watched him a moment longer.

But this felt deeper. She was no longer talking.

The river moved in its slow, endless way. Light flickered across its surface like a language neither of them could name.

And then Dan's breath slowed. He was pulling from deeper inside. The kind of breath that belonged to something no longer quite human.

Leona watched, staying close and bearing witness.

The scent of the river shifted.

It came to him not as a smell, but a feeling. A cool shimmer in the blood, a brightness in the chest. Something ancient and fluid, like laughter rising from below the surface.

Dan blinked once.

Then everything dropped away.

He didn't fall. He slid. Not down, but *through* as the world was thinning, stretching, and then reassembling around a center that was no longer human.

The cold was gone. Or maybe it was just irrelevant.

His body was motion. The pulse of the river all around him, part of him. He didn't think about what he was. He didn't *think* at all.

He *moved*.

Upstream, then down, slick and sharp. Twisting through current like it was a second skin. Pressure changed as he dove, his ears folding, muscles tucking. He didn't resist it. Didn't even command it. He simply *was* it.

There was a fish.

Somewhere close, just ahead. A flick of vibration through the water. It darted, he followed, missing it on purpose.

He broke the surface, rolled, and plunged again.

Every motion was a joy. Not a game, not a need. Joy, pure and present.

The river curved, narrowed, and opened again. Rocks jutted from below like teeth, and he slid between them effortlessly. A low branch grazed the surface, and he launched up to slap it with a forepaw, just because he *could*.

He could've kept going forever.

But something was still holding him, a connection.

Not a leash. Not a fear. Just... a thread. Faint, but steady.

It led backward—not in space, but in self.

He hesitated, treading water with a few lazy kicks.

Above, the wind rustled through cottonwoods. And somewhere at the edge of knowing, a shape stood by the riverbank. Watching. Waiting. Not calling him back, but... anchoring.

Dan turned once in the water, circled, then let himself drift to the surface.

And breathed.

Not like before.

But like return.

The water faded.

It didn't disappear, just released him, like a hand letting go of another.

Dan felt gravity return in increments. The ache of knees against stone. The cool air on skin. The steady thud of his own heart, recalibrating. He blinked.

He was crouched by the riverbank, exactly where he'd been. But everything had changed.

Leona hadn't moved.

She stood a few feet away, hands at her sides, not reaching, not retreating. Just watching.

Dan looked at her, then down at the water. A thin smile touched his mouth, reflexive and unguarded.

"That one was different," he said, voice quiet, like the sound might scare it away.

Leona's head tilted slightly. "I saw."

He exhaled, slow and full. There was a dampness along his collar that didn't come from the river, more like sweat burned clean.

"It wasn't like the others," he repeated. "The crow... that was fast and wild. I didn't have time to think."

She said nothing and chose to let him speak, or not.

"But this..." He looked toward the water again, the surface smooth now. "It felt right. Like the whole body knew what to do, and all it wanted was to move. Not escape. Not feed. Just... play."

He looked up at her again. There was no disbelief in her face. No judgment.

Only recognition.

She crouched beside him, not touching, but close enough he could feel her presence.

"They carry medicine," she said quietly. "Otters. In my culture. They remind us how to carry lightness even when things are heavy."

Dan nodded slowly. He didn't have words, not good ones. But that didn't matter.

She saw it in him anyway.

And for the first time since it all began, Dan sensed something he hadn't expected.

Not control.

Not power.

Belonging.

NINETEEN

THE MORNING AIR WAS WARMING. The kind of day that promised it was coming.

Dan moved slowly and deliberately. No rush. A clipboard in one hand, radio on his belt, and a trailhead sign in need of updating.

He parked at the Blacktail Creek pullout and stepped out, boots pressing into half-dry mud. Behind him, the land unfolded in soft layers with distant ridgelines brightening with the sun. The creek carved its way through low meadows; birds darted between willow thickets.

The sign stood just off the trail, weathered and leaning slightly. Dan walked over and studied the map under its warped plexiglass. A corner of it had yellowed where the seal failed. Someone had scratched initials low on the frame. A bear warning hung half-loose, flapping softly with each breeze.

Dan peeled it off, replaced it with a fresh one, and pressed the laminate flat. His hands moved out of habit, but his focus drifted.

Since the drive with Leona, the world felt more balanced—like it was slowly realigning.

He ran a hand along the wooden rail of the sign, then turned to look back toward the road.

A group of tourists had pulled in. Out-of-state plates and wide-brimmed hats. A kid dropped a bag of trail mix and stooped to grab it, spilling some without noticing the ant pile close by.

Dan watched, not with judgment—just with a kind of quiet detachment. He used to feel separate from these people. Now he wasn't sure if he was separate from *anything.*

Back at the truck, he flipped open his logbook and scribbled a short entry.

Blacktail Creek. Sign replaced. Trail condition drying.

He left the door open and leaned back in the driver's seat, letting the sun press onto his shoulder. The radio crackled faintly with ambient noise, Park Service check-ins, nothing for him.

Not yet.

The next stop was a half mile up a service road, gated off to keep the public out. Dan parked at the turn and walked in, some deadfall cracking underfoot.

The trail cam was strapped to a lodgepole just off a game path, where the undergrowth funneled wildlife between two low ridges. He'd set it a few weeks ago, mostly out of routine to spot elk, deer, and sometimes a lone black bear that wandered through the grove.

He unlatched the casing, popped the card, and slid it into the small reader he kept in his vest. The screen lit up with its usual blur of motion-capture stills: a bull elk passing at night, a fox in mid-step, two raccoons in a slow-motion standoff.

Then he paused.

A badger had moved into frame—broad, low, throwing dirt behind it in quick, practiced bursts. It worked the ground with its whole body, efficient and focused, the kind of animal that didn't waste effort.

Dan flipped to the next still. The badger had stopped digging. Its head was up, dirt on its snout, and it was looking straight at the lens.

Just... watching.

The next frame showed it turning back to the hole, returning to the task like nothing had happened.

Most animals ignored the camera. A few might flinch if it clicked too loud. But this, this was something else.

It hadn't looked like recognition, but it also hadn't looked random.

A glance. A pause. Awareness.

Dan exhaled through his nose and gave a small shake of his head, half smile on his lips. "Alright, then."

He saved the frame and slid the card back into the camera.

Nothing dramatic.

But it stayed with him.

Back at the truck, Dan poured the last of his coffee into the travel cup and climbed onto the front bumper, resting one boot against the tire. The sun warmed the metal beneath him, and the day had settled.

He reached behind the seat and pulled out his field glasses, the sturdy pair he kept tucked in a worn canvas case. He adjusted the focus with one hand until the landscape came clear in layers.

A small herd of elk grazed near the edge of the timber, mostly cows and yearlings, scattered but moving with loose cohesion. Farther out, something larger—a moose, maybe—moved through the willows with the slow, weightless gait of an animal that never hurries.

Dan stayed still.

There was something in the act of watching that soothed him now.

The radio clicked softly at his hip.

Wyatt's voice followed, easy and matter of fact.

"Dan, you around?"

Dan lowered the glasses slightly, eyes still on the horizon. "Go ahead."

"Are you up by Blacktail?"

"Close."

"Can you swing back toward the overlook above the hot springs? Got a few folks turned a little rowdy. Nothing major, just better with two of us."

Dan clicked the mic again. "Tourists?"

"No, locals," Wyatt replied. "Familiar faces. I know them. Sounds like they've been drinking a while—Steve Gregory, Jean Thomas, Candace Bright's one of them. Thought it might help to show up with a second uniform."

Dan didn't say anything right away. He remembered the name vaguely. Mentioned in passing during the school visit.

"Copy that," he said. "On my way."

He slid the field glasses back into their case, gave the land a last look, and stepped off the bumper. The door creaked as he climbed in. The truck rumbled to life, steady and familiar.

The overlook sat above a bend in the river where the water flattened out, wide and glassy, before curving south again. A low railing marked the edge of the turnout. On clear days, you could almost see Electric Peak.

Dan spotted Wyatt's truck first. It was parked at an angle, engine idling, the driver's door open. A small group stood nearby: four adults leaning against the rail, voices loud enough to carry, music blasting, their movements loose with drink.

As Dan pulled in beside the other truck, Wyatt stepped away from the group and met him halfway.

"Appreciate it," he said under his breath. "It's not bad. Just off enough that I didn't want to play it solo."

Dan nodded. "The locals you mentioned?"

"Yeah, folks from Gardiner."

They approached together, casual, not confrontational. The kind of body language that said *we're not here to ruin your afternoon, but we're not going to ignore it either.*

One of the men turned as they neared. Mid-forties, face pink with sun and something stronger, hand curled around a can of beer he wasn't bothering to hide.

"Well hell, the cavalry," he said, grinning. "Are we bothering someone?"

"Nope," Wyatt said evenly. "Just making sure the overlook doesn't turn into a bar."

A light laugh. "It's public land."

"Sure is," Dan said. "Which means everyone gets to feel safe using it."

That line landed just enough. Not aggressive. Just steady.

Candace glanced over her shoulder and took in Dan's uniform. She looked tired more than anything—sunken around the eyes, arms crossed tight across her chest. She didn't say a word.

Wyatt shifted to a lighter tone. "Tell you what. Why don't you finish that one," —he nodded toward the beer— "then head on back to town."

The group muttered among themselves. One man looked like he might push back, but Candace cut him off without speaking with just a look, firm and worn.

Dan stepped back a pace, letting Wyatt finish it off. Within a minute, the group was packing up. There was no fuss, no argument, just the slow shuffling of people who knew they'd been given the easy out.

When the truck door slammed, and the engine turned over, Wyatt exhaled.

"That could have gone worse," he said.

Dan watched the taillights disappear around the bend.

"They weren't looking for trouble," he said. "Just nowhere else to go."

Wyatt gave a small nod. "That's usually how it starts."

They stood in silence for a moment, looking out across the valley. The river gleamed under the soft light, and the ridgeline beyond it held its quiet shape.

"Did you catch anything interesting on camera this morning?" Wyatt asked.

Dan thought of the badger. The dirt on its snout. The way it looked into the lens.

"Yeah," he said. "One thing."

Wyatt stretched his back with a quiet grunt, then turned toward his truck. "I appreciate the backup. I owe you one."

Dan shook his head. "You'd do the same."

Wyatt gave a half-wave as he climbed in. A moment later he was easing down the road, dust trailing lightly behind.

Dan stayed a minute longer.

The overlook was quiet now. The river moved with slow certainty through the flat below, flashing silver where the light caught it.

He leaned on the rail, hands resting on the warm metal. A few birds stirred in the trees behind him. The world had steadied again. But that name, Candace Bright, lodged somewhere in the back of his mind.

Twenty

DAN WAS ALMOST HOME, his face windburned and his boots crusted with a fine red grit.

His phone buzzed as he pulled into the parking lot.

Leona: *Hey Dan—Justine Walsh (our VP) is organizing a hike for a few staff this Saturday. Small group, out near Tower. Interested?*

Another buzz.

Leona: *Also, no dogs allowed on trails, I know you know. Tell Shankley we owe him one.*

Dan grinned and rubbed the back of his neck. He'd let Shankley out of the apartment and he was sniffing his way across the edge of the lot.

Dogs weren't allowed on trails inside the park. Dan had recited the rule more times than he could count, along with the fire safety protocols and the bear awareness warnings. Still, he liked that she'd said it anyway.

He carefully typed the reply.

Dan: *Count me in. Let me know where to meet.*

There was a pause, and then:

Leona: *Trailhead meet-up at 8. I'll bring the coffee.*

Dan pocketed the phone. He'd been outside all day but the idea of a hike off the clock felt good.

Inside, Shankley looked up expectantly as Dan opened the door.

"Not this time, bud, I promise I'll make it up to you."

Shankley's tail wagged anyway. Dan wished he was as good at handling bad news.

The next morning, the trailhead was already warming when Dan pulled in. He spotted Leona first. She was crouched by the tailgate of her truck, retying the laces of a hiking boot. When she stood, she waved casually, as if they'd just run into each other at the grocery store.

"Morning, Ranger Nowak," she said with a crooked grin.

"Morning, Miss Windreed." He adjusted his cap. "I remember you said something about coffee?"

She held up a battered thermos in reply. "Of course I did. A promise is a promise."

Two people were milling near the trailhead sign, one older woman in a wide-brimmed hat and sunglasses, and a younger guy who looked like he'd been peeled off a climbing wall. The woman turned as they approached.

"Dan, this is Justine Walsh," Leona said. "Our vice-principal and fearless trail wrangler."

Justine offered a hand. "Thanks for coming. Leona said you might be up for some mid-spring meandering."

"Absolutely," Dan said, shaking her hand. "Nice to meet you."

The younger guy nodded from under a beanie. "Hey, I'm Evan. The new-ish Math teacher."

"Dan. Wildlife." He gave a small wave. "Still new myself."

They milled around for a while, adjusting packs and swapping pleasantries, nobody in a hurry to get going. Somewhere close by a few magpies squawked and squabbled.

Dan felt his shoulders ease. No uniform today. No radio clipped to his hip. Just boots and trail dust, exactly what he'd been missing.

Justine checked her watch, then looked around. "Alright, just us four today. It's an easy trail, out-and-back. If we're lucky, we might spot some bighorns on the far bluff. If we're *unlucky*, we'll run into middle schoolers on a field trip." She raised an eyebrow at Leona. "No offense."

"None taken," Leona said. "I brought snacks."

Dan fell into step beside her as they set off, the group spacing naturally with Evan and Justine ahead and Leona and Dan a few strides behind.

"Do you get out here much?" she asked as the trail narrowed.

"Some, more in off-hours. When it's quiet."

"It's always quiet if you hike with the right people."

Dan glanced over. She wasn't smiling, but her eyes held that same steady glint as before.

He looked forward again. The trail bent into a stand of lodgepole pine, the trunks straight and pale. The ground underneath cushioned his steps, still soft in early summer.

"Let's find out," he said.

As they walked the group naturally stretched. Justine and Evan had fallen quiet up ahead, their footsteps the only conversation. The trail cut across a dry hillside now, the pines thinning into open views of the valley below.

Dan adjusted his pack and glanced sideways. "Do you always hike with coworkers?"

"Well Principal Wallace gets a pass," Leona said. "But Justine's a great person. And Evan—well, he's still trying to figure out if Gardiner is purgatory or just a weirdly placed rest stop."

Dan chuckled. "I guess that depends on the day."

They walked a few paces before he added, "I used to hike more back in Colorado. Eagle County. I'd get up into the Flat Tops too when I could. Big skies. Old scars from the burn zones. It's honest country."

"Honest," Leona repeated, as if tasting the word.

He shrugged. "You can't fake a fire scar. Or the way the ground heals after it. Some trails seem to teach you how long things take."

Leona nodded. "Yeah. I get that."

She picked up a pebble from the trail. "It's Parent Night next week."

Dan glanced over. "You sound thrilled."

"Oh, absolutely." She gave a small, dry laugh. "It's the highlight of my year, the awkward conversations under fluorescent lighting. A table full of curriculum handouts no one reads."

"No wonder you needed a hike."

"I have this debate with myself every time," she said. "Is it a chance to build something? Or am I just going through the motions again?"

She tossed the pebble to the side of the trail. "Some parents come in looking for a partnership. Some come in looking for someone to blame."

Dan didn't say anything right away. The path narrowed slightly, and they stepped single file for a few paces before it opened again.

"Do you ever get one who surprises you?" he asked.

Leona smiled faintly. "Yeah. Sometimes. And I hang onto those."

Dan nodded. "In my old job, it was landowners. Same drill, some want help, some want a fight."

"Yeah, people can be a lot of work," she said.

They rounded a bend, and the bluff came into view, jagged and golden in the late morning sun. A hawk coasted the thermals above, wings tilting.

"Thanks for inviting me."

Leona gave a one-shoulder shrug. "You looked like someone who needed a trail."

They reached an open spot with a view and Leona paused and tapped Dan's arm lightly. "Let's have a quick break," she said, already loosening the straps on her pack.

Dan slipped his pack off, eyes scanning the slope beyond. Leona joined him, her thermos clinking gently as she dug it out of her bag.

"D'you always carry coffee up a mountain?"

"Always," she said, unscrewing the lid. "It's a ritual."

Dan smiled, stretching his legs. "Hard to argue with ritual."

From somewhere above, a raven croaked once, deep and rough, echoing like a bark through the trees.

Dan felt it before he heard it, a change in the rhythm of the trail.

Justine and Evan were up the trail, maybe a hundred yards ahead, out of view. Then came a startled shout—half-yelled, half-swallowed—and the unmistakable sound of retreating boots scuffing hard against dirt and stone.

Dan moved without thinking, stepping past Leona toward the sound, then froze.

A shape pushed through the timber.

A full-grown male grizzly.

Massive.

Shoulders rolling like coiled springs beneath fur the color of old wheat. The bear had clearly been disturbed, its head snapping as it changed direction, coming straight down the slope.

And then it saw them.

The bear halted, nostrils flaring, chest heaving. It was close, too close. Maybe thirty feet. Its ears weren't pinned, but its eyes locked on them with unmistakable force.

Dan slowly lifted one arm, signaling Leona to stay still. "Don't move," he murmured. "Don't run."

Leona didn't.

She didn't move. She didn't run.

She *bowed her head slightly.*

And then, barely audible, she whispered.

"Mitákuye Oyás'iŋ."

Dan caught the words but didn't react. His own training took over as he held his ground, avoided eye contact, kept his body square but not threatening.

The bear huffed once. Deep and low. A blast of breath that raised the dust at its feet.

Dan felt something stir in return—not fear, more a raw awareness. The bear looked straight at him, held him in its gaze for the space of a breath.

It wasn't assessing. It wasn't afraid. It was just there.

Then, as suddenly as it had come, the bear exhaled, turned, and shouldered its way back into the trees. The brush shivered in its wake.

For a long moment, neither of them spoke.

Leona was the first to break the silence. She turned to Dan slowly, her face calm but searching. "That was... different."

Dan's eyes were still on the trees. "That could've gone bad. We're lucky it didn't."

"It felt like you were there with it," she said.

He shook his head. "It clocked us and made a choice. That's all."

Leona studied him. "You felt it though. That—something."

He met her eyes, then looked away. "Just a bear encounter that didn't go wrong."

Leona said nothing. She simply nodded and, noticing the coffee still in her hand, took a sip. Dan felt her watching him, not with suspicion but with recognition.

Behind them, Justine and Evan reappeared, wide-eyed and shaken but intact. Evan let out a laugh. "Jesus, that scared the crap out of me."

The trail narrowed again as they descended, the bear encounter still clinging to the air like smoke. They stayed closer to Justine and Evan now with unspoken consensus, but the real shift was between them.

Their conversation had slipped into something quieter, stripped of small talk. No more commentary on the weather, or coffee jokes. The silence held a different weight.

Leona adjusted the strap of her pack and said, almost offhand, "I grew up on a reservation. South Dakota, the Cheyenne River."

Dan glanced over, surprised—not at the admission, but at the way she said it. Straightforward and without the push to explain more.

"My people are Lakota," she continued. "My grandmother used to say *Mitákuye Oyás'iŋ* before we went to sleep, the same words I said to the bear."

Dan nodded, waiting.

"It means 'All my relations.' But not like cousins or uncles." She paused, stepping carefully over a rock, then looked at him. "It means everything. The trees, the wind, the bear. You. Me. All connected."

Dan didn't respond right away. He thought about the bear's eyes, the shared breath. The grounded, unmistakable presence of it.

"That's a powerful way to walk through the world," he said finally.

"It is," she said. "But it's also just... how I was taught to see."

They kept walking, the trail soft beneath their boots. The others were just ahead; voices faint but grounding.

Dan didn't speak, giving Leona her space, her rhythm. But after a few more steps, words came—low, almost more to the trail than to her.

"I didn't grow up with that kind of teaching," he said. "Kansas. Flat land, rows of wheat. A Lutheran father and mom who worked nights at the clinic. Good people. Practical. The kind that believe in hard work and not much else."

Leona looked over, listening but not interrupting.

"We didn't talk about connection. Or the land, really. Except when it needed mowing. Or when a storm ruined a season's yield." He gave a dry smile. "I guess my worldview came from weather reports and school assembly rules."

They walked a little farther, boots crunching on the trail.

"I used to think the natural world was something you managed. Controlled. Like fences and gates and wildlife tags could actually hold back the wild."

Dan looked ahead where Justine was shifting bear spray from her pack to her pocket.

Leona didn't say anything, but he could feel her watching him again. She was listening for something deeper than the words.

"I don't know what I believe now," Dan said. "But I know there's more than what I was taught."

Leona walked a few steps before responding. Her voice was steady, but soft enough to keep it between them.

"In our tradition, we watch animals. Not just for what they do, but how they live. How they move through the world." She glanced at him. "They know things we've forgotten or choose to push down."

Dan looked ahead, the trail easing into a shallow curve. A chipmunk darted across the path and vanished into the underbrush.

"It's not your fault," she said. "How you were taught. Most people are raised in ways that separate them from the land. From each other. From themselves, sometimes."

Dan didn't argue. He couldn't.

"But there are other ways," Leona added.

Dan nodded slowly. "Kinda feels like I'm starting from scratch."

Leona smiled, not unkindly. "Everyone is. The trick is figuring out what's worth keeping."

They kept walking, and the trees grew thicker again, the light slanting gold through the canopy. The air felt richer somehow—quieter, but full.

She didn't say more, but something hung there between them: maybe the old ways weren't just stories.

Maybe they were tracks you could still follow. And perhaps there was still time to learn how to read them.

By the time they reached the trailhead again, the day had tilted into early afternoon.

Justine and Evan were already peeling off gear, talking low and a little too fast, like they were still coming down from the adrenaline. Evan offered a shaky laugh as he opened his car door, and Justine clapped him on the shoulder before heading to her truck.

Dan loosened his pack straps and let it drop to the gravel. His back ached, but in a good way—earned. Leona stood beside him, sipping the last of her coffee, eyes back up the trail where the bear had disappeared hours before.

"How's the trail coffee holding up?" Dan asked.

She gave him a sideways smile and they shared a glance—steady, longer than before.

Then Leona nodded once, turned, and headed toward her truck.

Dan watched her go, then looked back at the trail. The dust had settled, but the path still held their prints.

TWENTY-ONE

LEONA STOOD IN FRONT OF THE MIRROR in the staff bathroom, smoothing the sleeves of her charcoal blouse. It was simple, neat, and deliberately non-political. She glanced at the silver and turquoise band on her wrist, briefly considering whether to remove it. She'd pulled her hair back into a low ponytail, a touch severe, but it would have to do.

Parent Night.

The phrase itself made her jaw tighten.

Out in the hallway, the muffled sounds of chairs scraping into place and laughter echoed off the tile. She could picture the other teachers chatting in small groups, comparing notes on attendance, on last year's drama, whether any parents would show up drunk.

She adjusted her necklace, a slim piece of slate on a cord, and took a breath. In. Out.

Justine Walsh had reminded everyone, again, to "keep it open, warm, and constructive."

Leona had smiled politely.

The truth was, Parent Night always left her split in two. She'd grown used to the unspoken question that hung in some parents' eyes: *What exactly are you teaching them?*

She walked back to her classroom, the fluorescent lights humming overhead. Her tables were arranged in a loose circle, handouts laid out in tidy stacks: curriculum overview, reading list, upcoming projects. Ordinary and reassuring.

The jar of hard candies on the back table had been Justine's suggestion.

She stood by the door as parents filtered in, a few familiar faces, a few polite smiles, some stiff nods. Most looked tired. Some looked wary.

A couple introduced themselves quickly and moved on. One man said, "You're the one who takes them out into the park, right? I think that's—different."

* * *

Leona smiled with her mouth but not her eyes. "It's part of the curriculum. Observation and awareness."

He gave a thumbs up. "I support it. Just make sure you keep them from wandering off?" And then he laughed like he'd said something funny.

A few parents hovered near the back, flipping through the handouts. Leona caught a quick glance from one of the mothers before she leaned close to another and said something too softly to hear. There was a brief laugh, the kind that wasn't meant to carry. Leona fought to keep her gaze away from the two women.

Out in the hallway she caught sight of Mr. Wallace, working the room, shaking hands, smiling with ease, leaning in as if everything being said to him mattered deeply. He was an old hand at dealing with parents. He understood the optics, and Leona supposed that is what it took to make Principal.

When he turned and caught her eye, the smile lingered just a second too long. Not warm. Not cold either. A reminder that she represented the school.

Leona gave a small nod. A quiet agreement to stay on script.

Trust, in this place, was something to be earned twice and doubted once.

Leona kept her face neutral. She knew how to absorb those moments without showing the bruise.

She moved through the evening with practiced ease. Her voice was even, her tone calm. She talked about primary sources and land history, about incorporating field experiences into the writing process.

It was nearly the end of the hour when she noticed Star sitting in the far corner, alone. No parent at her side.

Leona blinked, she hadn't seen her come in.

Star looked smaller than usual. There was a stillness in her, that coiled quietly, like she was listening for something no one else could hear.

Their eyes met across the room.

Leona offered a small nod. Star didn't return it, not exactly. But she didn't look away either.

The crowd thinned as the hour wound down, parents trickling out, murmuring their goodnights. A few lingered by the display case in the hall, pretending to study student art while really just finishing their small talk.

Leona stood by the window, sipping the dregs of lukewarm coffee from a paper cup. The fluorescent light buzzed faintly overhead. Outside, the last of the sunlight caught in the flagpole cable, making it shiver.

She didn't feel angry, just hollow in that particular way this night always brought. Like she'd poured out more of herself than anyone had asked for, and still somehow not enough.

In another life, this kind of evening might've felt like community. Here, it was something else. A performance with the house lights on.

She turned back to the room, eyes instinctively drifting toward the corner where Star still sat, silent and unmoving.

"Star," Leona said gently, as if they were already in the middle of a conversation. "Are you hanging back for a reason?"

Star looked up, her expression unreadable but alert. "I figured the parents would clear out eventually."

Leona crossed her arms, leaned lightly against the desk across from her. "You didn't bring your mom."

"She's not big on these things," Star said. "She said they're a waste of time."

Leona gave a small nod. "But you came anyway."

Star shrugged, but it wasn't careless. "Well, I didn't come for her."

Leona let that sit for a moment.

"I wanted to hear how you explain about us to them," Star said, her voice low but clear. "If it's the same as what you tell us. I hoped it would be."

That registered. Leona's gaze sharpened—not with offense, but with something closer to respect.

"Fair question," she said. "And?"

"It was close," Star said, after a beat. "You edited a little. But I get why."

Leona couldn't hide a faint smile. "You're right about that."

Star looked down at her hands. "She thinks I'm wasting time on things that don't matter. The stories. The old stuff. Says this won't help me get anywhere."

"But you don't agree."

Star met her eyes. "No. I think it's the only part that *does* matter."

Leona studied her, heart ticking just a little harder in her chest. She remembered being that age. Working hard at school when nobody cared.

"You said something," Star went on. "In class. About the land remembering but you didn't really explain it."

"I didn't want to flatten it into something easy," Leona said. "Some things are meant to be considered rather than solved."

Star leaned back, thoughtful. "My grandfather used to talk like that, before he passed, but my mom doesn't talk like that."

Leona watched her for a long moment, then pushed off the desk.

"You remind me of someone I knew," she said. "Smart. Stubborn. Saw things others missed."

Star raised an eyebrow. "Is that a compliment?"

Leona smiled. "Well, that depends on who you ask."

She moved to the bookshelf behind her desk. After a moment, she pulled out a slim volume with well-thumbed pages marked with pencil. There was no title on the cover. Just a plain wrap and a faint water stain in the corner.

"This isn't required reading," she said, handing it over. "But it's one of the books I like to come back to."

Star turned the book in her hands, curious but cautious.

"There's a part in there," Leona added, "about standing in two places at once. Not quite belonging in either. It's something that has always stuck with me."

Star looked up, more exposed than she'd probably meant to be.

"I'm not trying to fix anything," Leona said gently. "But if you ever want to talk about what you're feeling... I'll listen."

Star gave a small, guarded nod. The kind that meant *maybe.*

She turned to leave, the book tucked under one arm, her other pushed deep into her pocket.

* * *

The diner sat on the edge of Gardiner, half-lit and half-empty, its windows throwing long reflections onto the parking lot. Inside, Leona scanned the tables, pleased to see no middle school parents had made it their next stop .

She slid into the booth across from Dan and exhaled like she'd been holding her breath since the school doors closed. Pulling her hair loose from the ponytail, she let it fall over her shoulders.

Dan closed the menu. "You look like someone who survived something."

Leona gave him a look, then smirked. "Parent Night. Ancient ritual of mutual misunderstanding."

He smiled and they chatted for a while.

The waitress came by—two waters, late plates ordered without much thought. When she left, Leona rested her hands on the warm water cup and stared into it for a while before speaking again.

"Star came by tonight without her mom. She's mixed race, you know."

Dan nodded. "I guessed that."

"She's not sure what to do with it yet. Or maybe she is, and the rest of the world's not ready." She looked up at him. "It's complicated, being from two places that don't always speak to each other."

Dan was quiet but he pursed his lips in a kind of quiet understanding.

"I get it," she added. "Not in the same way. But I get it."

"Growing up on a reservation?" he asked, gently.

Leona nodded. "I left when I was seventeen."

"What made you leave?"

She hesitated, then smiled slightly. "Someone who could see me. Martha. She taught at the tribal college, but she'd spent most of her adult life off reservation. She still came back, always came back." Leona paused. "She didn't tell me to leave, but she just... asked if I'd thought about what leaving might look like. And if I had the courage to make a path where one didn't already exist."

Dan leaned in a little. "You still talk to her?"

"Now and then. She's in Bozeman and she used to teach. But I think she mostly does advocacy work now." Leona traced a line in the condensation on her glass. "I think about her more than I call her."

Dan nodded. He could tell she wasn't just talking about a mentor. She was talking about a connection—something that stitched the past to the present, however imperfectly.

"Did it ever feel like walking away?" he asked.

Leona looked out the window for a long moment before answering. "Sometimes. But only when I'm looking back from someone else's idea of who I'm supposed to be."

Their food arrived, the quiet clatter of plates giving them a pause. Outside, the wind picked up, stirring dust in the parking lot. A passing semi threw its lights across the booth before disappearing up the road.

Dan sipped his water. "Do you ever wish you'd stayed?"

Leona shook her head.

She didn't speak again right away. Her eyes followed a moth that fluttered against the window glass, briefly caught in the glow of the overhead light.

"Sometimes I think about what it would've meant if I had," she said. "What I might've learned by staying. What I might've missed."

She traced a slow arc on the side of her glass with her thumb.

"There's this idea that leaving is breaking away. And staying is loyalty. But it's not that simple. You can stay and still feel lost. Or leave and still keep everything with you. The parts that matter anyway."

She looked at him then, steady.

"So no, I don't wish I'd stayed. But I don't think I ever really left, either."

Twenty-Two

The sun was just beginning to warm the western edge of Mammoth when Dan heard a half bark from Shankley at the apartment door. Not a warning, more like a greeting. He found the dog wagging its tail, his nose pressed against the screen.

Leona stood on the stoop, hands in her pockets, her braided hair tucked into the collar of a faded canvas jacket. "Are you ready?" she asked.

Dan opened the door wider. "He is."

Shankley pushed past Dan and pressed his shoulder into Leona's legs like they were old friends. She scratched behind his ears without hesitation.

"I think I've been accepted," she said, crouching to meet him properly.

Dan watched, a little amused. "I guess he senses you're a dog person. He usually takes more than a minute to get acquainted."

"Maybe I don't feel like a stranger."

Dan smiled at that. "You want coffee before we go?"

"Nope. You're buying me one on the road."

They walked together out to the lot where Dan and Leona's Tacomas were parked side by side, both coated in a fine dusting of pollen. The vehicles looked like they belonged to the same kind of life with faded paint and pitted windshields.

Leona eyed his truck, then hers. "So, whose chariot?"

Dan shrugged. "Yours is cleaner."

"Yours has better tires."

"She pulls to the left."

"I've got a loose tailgate."

Shankley sat down between them, ears perked, as if waiting to cast the deciding vote.

Dan looked down at him. "What do you think, buddy?"

Shankley got up, turned once, and hopped into the open passenger side of Leona's truck like the matter had been settled days ago.

Leona smirked. "That's a vote if I've ever seen one."

Dan opened the driver's side door for her. "All yours, then."

"Careful," she said, sliding in. "I don't let just anyone ride shotgun."

Dan tossed his pack into the back and climbed in. The cab smelled familiar—faintly of Leona. Shankley curled in behind the seats with a satisfied huff.

They had the windows cracked halfway, letting the cool morning air thread through the cab. The road unwound ahead of them in long curves and sudden dips, dust rising in the rearview.

For a while, they didn't talk. A silence that grows when two people trust the landscape to do the talking.

Dan leaned one elbow on the window, eyes scanning the roadside.

"Keep watch," he said after a few miles. "This stretch sometimes pulls surprises."

"Like what?" Leona asked, glancing sideways.

"Had a mountain lion cross once. Middle of the day. Looked right at me like I was the one out of bounds."

A few minutes passed. They rounded a bend where the trees opened briefly to marshland, shallow water pooling among willows. Shankley's ears twitched behind them, and Dan slowed instinctively.

"There," he said, pointing just off the shoulder.

A moose stood in the water up to its knees, its massive shoulders rising from the reeds like some forgotten thing. Dark fur soaked and dripping, long face lowered toward the shallows.

"Bull," Dan murmured. "Young one. Probably two, three years."

Leona leaned forward, hands on the dash. "It's huge."

"Moose always look half-made until you see one up close, then you realize it's built like a mountain with legs."

They watched it for a moment, unmoving.

Leona tilted her head. "Isn't it just a goofy looking elk?"

Dan smiled. "Not exactly."

Leona shifted the truck into park. The engine ticked in the stillness.

"Elk are fast, lean, and travel in groups. Nervous energy. Moose are slower. Solitary. Less likely to run, but more likely to hold their ground. You push too close, they don't warn you like a bear. They just come at you."

"Sounds familiar," Leona said, a wry look passing across her face.

Dan glanced at her. "You saying I've got moose energy?"

"I'm saying it's pretty clear that you don't move unless you mean to."

He didn't argue. The moose lifted its head briefly, water trailing from its beard, then turned and disappeared into the willows like it had never been there at all.

They sat a moment longer before Leona shifted the truck back into drive.

"Good omen," he said.

"For who?" Leona asked.

"We'll find out."

They drove on, the road rising gently as the terrain began to change to more rock, more slope, and the scent of pine sharpening the air. The canyon was getting closer. You could feel it even before you saw it.

They pulled into the lot near Artist Point mid-morning, the sun beginning to climb higher in the clear sky. A handful of tourists were already gathered near the overlook, their voices whispering, as if they'd wandered into some ancient cathedral.

They parked beneath a wind-stunted pine. Shankley stirred in the back but didn't make a move to get out—just rested his chin on the seat, eyes alert.

"You staying put?" Dan asked over his shoulder.

The dog gave a soft grunt, as if to say he'd rather not deal with crowds.

Dan reached back to scratch between his ears. "Good call."

Leona grabbed her sunglasses and they stepped out into the light.

The sound hit them first—a distant, constant roar, like wind filtered through stone. The Lower Falls of the Yellowstone River.

They walked the short trail to the overlook, the heat of the day already building on the exposed rock. At the railing, the canyon opened before them—sheer walls of rust, ochre, sulfur-yellow, and soft white streaked. The river boiled in the far depths, glint and fury, threading itself through the canyon below.

Dan leaned against the rail, eyes tracing the curves of the canyon. "You don't get it from the photos," he said. "The scale."

Leona nodded slowly. "It feels ancient."

"I was reading about the geology of it," he said after a pause. "The canyon. The falls."

Leona glanced at him. "Yeah?"

"The whole thing's been reshaped over and over. Massive eruptions, then ice, then steam. It didn't happen once. It kept changing and still is."

He pointed toward the far wall, where steam curled faintly from a vent just below the rim.

"They think the yellow rock formed from hydrothermal fluids—heat rising through the fractures, altering the stone from the inside out."

He paused, then added, "It wasn't carved by one force. It took fire, water, and time."

Leona looked at him then—not surprised, listening more to the tone than the words.

Dan shifted his weight slightly. "The Shoshone lived here. Others passed through and hunted here. Some tribes say this place is alive—aware even."

Leona smiled faintly. "Those aren't just stories."

Dan nodded. He was quiet for a long moment, then said, "Back in the Eagle office, it was all diagrams and permits. Animal counts and resource maps. But I think I missed something. I think I was walking through all this without ever really seeing it."

They stood close together, the wind brushing their sleeves.

"I used to think places like this just happened," he said. "Now I think they're still happening."

Leona reached into her jacket pocket, pulled out a small pouch of tobacco, and held it lightly in her palm. She didn't speak, didn't make a show of it.

Dan recognized the tobacco talisman.

Behind them, the murmur of voices from the overlook drifted in and out. A raven lifted off from a nearby ledge, wings pulling hard against the updraft. It circled once overhead, then disappeared into the canyon.

Leona turned to him. "Let's walk a bit."

They stepped back from the rail, away from the edge, away from the crowd.

They followed a narrow trail away from the overlook, where the canyon's roar softened behind them. The crowds thinned, then disappeared altogether. Only the wind remained, threading through lodgepole pines, bringing with it the cool scent of stone and bark.

They circled back to the truck, where Shankley sat up in the back seat as soon as Dan approached. His tail thumping.

"You ready?" Dan asked.

He cracked the door and clipped on the leash. Shankley jumped down and gave Leona a look of casual approval, like this had been the plan all along.

She gave his ears a quick scratch. "You're a wise one, huh?"

"He's good on the leash when he has to," Dan said. "Although he's not always one to follow the rules."

They moved back toward the trail, settling into an easy rhythm, Leona and Dan side by side, Shankley slightly ahead, his gait light and steady.

The ground was dry underfoot, pine needles layered thick in places, muffled their steps. The air smelled of warm resin and dust.

"I used to come out here as a kid," Leona said quietly. "When we visited. My uncle worked in construction near Cody for a while. We'd drive into the park, pull over at any spot that looked good, just sit and watch. It didn't matter if we saw anything. The watching part was the point."

Dan nodded but didn't speak. He understood that now in a way he hadn't before.

They walked a little further, trees opening to a high ridge with a low stone wall—built decades ago. Beyond it, the canyon returned, this time without rails or viewpoints. Just the raw edge of the world.

They stopped there. Shankley sat down beside Dan, leash slack between them.

Leona rested both hands on the stone, her gaze tracking the far wall of the canyon.

"In our tradition," she said, "there's something called *hanblečeya.* A vision quest. It's not a metaphor—you fast, you pray, and you go out alone, sometimes for days."

Dan listened, still and focused.

"It's not about asking the universe for clarity," she said. "It's about being seen. By the land. By the spirits. Sometimes, by the animals."

Dan recognized her words as he looked out at the folds of rock, their edges softened by distance. "Have you ever done it?"

She nodded. "Once before I left home."

"What happened?"

She paused, then said simply, "I wasn't alone."

Dan absorbed that. "Animal?"

Leona didn't answer right away. "In those moments, animals don't show up as symbols. Not like in a dream dictionary. They come because they're meant to. They stay as long as they need to. Sometimes they say nothing. Sometimes you understand them anyway."

Dan took time, considering the words. Then he said, "When it happens to me, I don't see anything. I just—slip.

"Slip my skin.

"It's like taking off a jacket and realizing there was something underneath the whole time."

Leona turned to him. "Does it hurt?"

"No," he said. "It was startling at first. But since, it's felt more natural than anything else I do."

She held his gaze for a moment longer. "Then it's real."

Dan leaned on the stone, arms folded, eyes down. "You think it's dangerous?"

"Yes," she said without hesitation. "But not in the way most people mean. It's not dangerous because it's unnatural. It's dangerous because it's sacred."

Dan looked at her. Waiting.

"You're not borrowing something," she said. "You're *entering* something. And once you enter, it knows you."

She turned back toward the canyon. The breeze lifted a strand of her hair across her cheek.

"Predators," she added, quieter now. "They're powerful allies. But they carry deep knowledge. And they also know hunger."

Dan watched the canyon, the way the light slanted off the stone. He hesitated before speaking, "So do people."

Leona turned to him, eyebrows raised, not in disagreement, just listening.

"I mean—humans," he added. "We carry deep knowledge too. But we forget. Or we use it for the wrong things. Sometimes I think we're the most dangerous animals of all."

Leona didn't respond right away. The wind shifted. A hawk circled high above the river, motionless but moving.

"We've done damage," Dan said. "I've seen it up close. Not just the big things like pollution and extinction, but smaller things too. Roads cut through migration paths. People feeding bears because they want a photo. For some reason, we assume it's all here for us."

He shifted his weight, looking down at Shankley, who blinked up at him like he already knew.

"I don't think our hunger is any less real, just less honest."

Leona studied him, then nodded once, slowly. "You're right."

They took the long way back, looping through a quieter stretch of forest where the trees thinned and the trail leaned again toward the canyon's edge. Shankley walked on the leash, sniffing the air with soft purpose. The breeze had picked up.

As they reached the final bend before the overlook, the sound returned— the steady, guttural roar of the falls. Deep and constant. Something you felt in your chest as much as you heard.

They'd stopped just short of the main viewpoint, standing a little off the trail where the trees opened and the canyon curved like a vast stone lung.

Dan looked out over the canyon at the churning, endless rush of water that had shaped this place.

Leona stepped closer to the edge, not recklessly, just with the calm of someone who didn't need to be told where the danger was.

"This place has always changed," she said, more to the air than to him. "It becomes what it was supposed to and then changes again."

Dan nodded, the words settling against him.

They stayed a moment longer, letting the roar surround them. Then Leona gave a soft whistle, and Shankley turned back, ready to go.

Dan followed, leash loose in his hand, boots brushing dust as they made their way up the slope.

TWENTY-THREE

LEONA LEANED AGAINST THE DOORFRAME of the ranger office, her shoulder brushing the peeling pine trim. Inside, Dan was at the small table near the window, flipping through a binder of wildlife data. Wyatt sat at the desk, feet propped on a half-open drawer, sipping something lukewarm from a Yellowstone mug.

"I've got a field trip planned next week," Leona said. "Just my class. I'm thinking of taking them down toward the canyon rim and doing the loop trail."

Wyatt looked up over the rim of his mug. "You're dragging 'em all the way out there?"

"They need it," Leona said. "Too much time indoors and too many worksheets. They've forgotten what ground feels like."

Dan glanced up from the binder. "Are you taking the whole class?"

"Twenty-two," she said. "Give or take the ones who fake being sick that morning."

Wyatt exchanged a look with Dan, then said, "We're scheduled for wildlife talks next week. Down at the small amphitheater just off the trailhead near Glen Creek. It could work to coordinate something."

Dan nodded. "It was supposed to be for walk-ins and tourists mostly, but it might be nice to have a real audience."

Leona raised an eyebrow. "Are you volunteering to teach my kids?"

Wyatt grinned. "More like inviting you to crash our party. We could cover the predator-prey talk—kids always appreciate that. Maybe track signs or scat too, something useful."

"You'd have to check with Rita," Dan added, more cautious. "She's big on the calendar not turning into a mess."

"I'll run it by her," Wyatt said, setting his mug down. "But I think she'd be good with it. The next generation seems important to her."

Leona nodded, thoughtful. "Could work. But if you tell them grizzly scat smells like pine trees, I'm pulling rank."

Dan smirked. "Fair enough."

* * *

The hum of the overhead lights mixed with the rustle of backpacks and pencil cases. Leona stood at the front of the room, one hand on the whiteboard marker, the other resting on the edge of her desk. Behind her, she'd drawn a rough outline of Yellowstone with rivers curling like blue veins and ridgelines sketched in charcoal streaks.

"All right," she said. "Next Thursday, we're heading out. Early start, be on the bus by 7:45. Please pack your own lunch, wear layers, and if I see anyone in flip-flops, you're staying behind with Principal Wallace."

There was a groan from the back. Someone muttered, "Even if it's hot?"

Leona pointed the marker at them without turning. "Especially if it's hot."

A few quiet laughs rippled through the room.

She capped the pen and stepped aside. "We'll be near Glen Creek. Ranger Keller and Ranger Nowak will be giving a short talk—mostly on wildlife tracking, predator-prey stuff. You'll get a chance to ask questions. Real questions. Not how many bears they've punched."

More laughter.

She scanned the room. "This isn't just a field trip to kill a day. I want you to be present. Take it in. Smell the air, notice things. Ask why they're important."

Star, seated two desks from the front, had her hands folded neatly on her notebook. She wasn't smiling, but she was listening. Leona saw that.

Across the room, a pair of girls exchanged whispers. One of them glanced at Star, then quickly looked away when Star met her eyes.

Leona's voice softened. "Nature can be a teacher if you let it. Ears and eyes open, you're sure to learn something."

Then someone asked if they'd see a wolf, and the moment moved on.

* * *

The bus rattled over the uneven road, suspension groaning with every dip. Students jostled in their seats, sharing earbuds and trading snacks. The energy was restless—the kind that comes with anticipation of a day out of the classroom.

Sitting near Star, a small girl named Ruby clutched her backpack to her chest, her shoulders tight. She hadn't said much all morning. One of the bigger boys across the aisle leaned over and made a snide comment—not loud, but loud enough.

Star turned in her seat, slow and deliberate.

"That's enough," she said, not sharp, just steady. "She didn't ask for your opinion."

The boy blinked, shrugged, and turned away.

Star looked at Ruby, then reached into her own bag and pulled out a small packet of dried fruit.

"Do you like mango?" she asked, holding it out.

Ruby hesitated, then nodded and took it with both hands.

"It's one of my favorites too," Star said, turning back toward the front, though she stayed angled slightly in her seat.

The bus hissed as it braked, the engine idled for a moment, then cut off. A sudden quiet settled over the parking area, broken only by wind moving through dry grass and the distant churn of water down in the canyon.

Leona stood and turned toward the students. "Okay. Start slowly. Stay in pairs. Don't wander until I say. And yes, we'll eat soon."

A chorus of groans and the clatter of backpacks followed as they funneled off the bus. Dan and Wyatt were already waiting near the edge of the clearing, uniforms neat, radios clipped to their belts. Dan had his hands in his pockets.

Leona walked over, nodded. "Thanks for doing this."

Dan gave a half-smile. "It was either this or counting duck chicks."

Wyatt added, "Now I think about it, maybe it's pretty much the same thing."

Star moved down from the bus near the back and stepped out, her boots landing softly on the gravel. Behind her, Ruby hesitated at the top step, still clutching her backpack.

Without turning, Star reached back with a gentle touch on Ruby's wrist. Ruby blinked, then followed.

They walked the rest of the way together—not side by side, exactly, but close enough to whisper, Ruby moving the backpack over one shoulder.

The students milled nearby, eyeing the rangers with varying degrees of interest and boredom.

The amphitheater wasn't much; a crescent of weathered logs set into the slope beneath a scrim of lodgepole pine. The students spread out in loose clumps, some sitting, others standing behind the benches. A few kicked at the dirt or looked away toward the edge of the trail.

Wyatt stepped up first. "Welcome to Glen Creek," he said. "You're officially outside the school zone now, so if you learn anything, it's entirely accidental."

A few kids laughed. One mimed applause. Wyatt grinned, let it hang a second, then pointed to the trees behind him. "This area's got a little of everything—bear, fox, coyote, mountain lion. And wolves, sometimes. Though you're more likely to see their prints than the animal itself."

Dan stepped forward, a canvas bag slung over one shoulder. "We thought we'd talk a little about predators—how they move through this land, how we track them, and why they matter."

He crouched, pulling out a set of rubber molds—tracks pressed in hardened casting material. He set them in a line on a flat patch of earth and began sketching alongside them with a stick. A wide pad, four toes, claws.

"Does anyone have a guess on what this is?"

"Dog," someone offered, a little too sure.

"Close," Dan said. "But not quite. Look at the claw marks."

There was a beat of silence before a voice near the back spoke up, low but certain.

"Wolf," Star said.

Dan nodded. "Exactly. Wolves usually leave a tighter print, claws just visible if the ground's soft. Dogs, especially pets, tend to splay more."

He moved down the line. "This one?"

"Fox?"

"Right. Notice how clean it is—almost dainty. Foxes weigh so little their prints barely register in dry ground. Sometimes we only know they passed by because mice stop moving."

That got a murmur. Dan glanced up.

“Predators shape everything around them,” he said. “Not just by what they kill, but how other animals behave because of them. Elk don’t linger in open meadows the same way when they know wolves are nearby. Even grass changes, because grazers move more.”

Wyatt stepped in again. “You might’ve heard of the trophic cascade. Sounds complicated, but all it means is when one species changes, especially a predator, it can set off a chain reaction. Not just in what gets eaten, but in how the whole landscape behaves.”

He gestured toward the trees. “Take wolves. When they were gone from Yellowstone, elk had no reason to move, so they stayed near streams, overgrazed the young willows and aspens, and slowly those trees disappeared. Birds lost nesting spots. Riverbanks began to erode.”

He paused. “But when the wolves came back, elk started moving again. Trees grew back. Beavers returned. Water flowed differently. The presence of a single predator—just a handful of wolves—reshaped an entire ecosystem.”

Dan added, “Most places don’t get to see that happen anymore. Yellowstone’s one of the few. The system’s not perfect, but it’s alive. And the wolves helped wake it up.

He glanced at the group

“We’re not trying to turn you into trackers,” Dan said. "Just help you to understand that the land leaves signs. And every sign has meaning.”

He picked up one of the molds, held it up.

"Wolves don't show up to scare people. They show up because they belong here. If you want to understand the land, you have to accept who lives on it, and why."

There was a brief silence. One of the students adjusted their hood. A girl near the front scribbled something in a notebook.

Star knelt near the edge of the bench, eyes focused, not just on the track, but the way Dan spoke about it. She didn't smile or nod, but she was listening harder than anyone else there.

Leona noticed. So did Dan.

Wyatt glanced at the group. "Let's go see if we can find something for real."

Leona added, "Short loop trail. Stay close and keep your eyes open."

There were a few mumbles, but the rangers had done their work. The kids were moving differently—quieter and more aware.

The group filed toward the trailhead, but Star hung back for a second. She looked once more at the wolf print mold, then down at the dirt sketch beneath it. With the edge of her boot, she brushed it gently, just enough to blur the outline.

They followed a narrow path that wound through the lodgepoles, needles soft underfoot. The air was cool, edged with the scent of resin. Dan walked ahead with Wyatt, pointing out fresh scat near a tree stump, a faint scratch mark on the bark.

Leona stayed at the back, eyes scanning the students. Most had settled into pairs.

Star trailed near the back—not lagging, just unhurried. She was watching the trees more than the other kids. Every so often she stopped, crouched to study something half-hidden under the brush—a twisted feather, a faint print in damp soil.

Behind her, a few students whispered. Not loud enough for most to hear—but just enough.

"Look at Bright," one boy muttered. "Natural tracker, right? Don't all her folks grow up doing this stuff?"

A few soft chuckles. One girl added, "Must be in the blood."

Star didn't turn. Didn't blink.

She straightened slowly and kept walking, eyes fixed ahead. She didn't rush. Just moved forward like the comment hadn't touched her. But Leona, ten feet back, caught the tension in her shoulders, a breath held a moment too long.

The trail opened into a small clearing. The group paused there, students scattering slightly to explore. Star walked to the edge, where a smooth boulder overlooked a narrow ravine cut by spring runoff.

She stood there for a long minute.

The others stayed behind, noise and motion fading into the trees.

Star crouched, ran her fingers along the moss clinging to the shaded side of the stone. A single ant moved across her knuckle. She watched it go.

When Leona joined her, she didn't say anything.

"Do you see the track?" Star asked after a bit, pointing to a crescent in the soft soil.

"Deer," Leona said.

Star nodded. "It came through alone."

Star stayed there, crouched low, fingers still pressed to the moss.

Leona stayed quiet for a long moment.

"I know someone," she said softly. "Someone I think you might want to meet."

Star didn't turn. Just looked out at the treetops swaying across the canyon.

"Who?" she asked.

Leona gave the smallest smile. "Let's just say—she knows how to listen."

TWENTY-FOUR

THE ROAD TWISTED through the back edge of Gardiner, past faded trailers and patchy fences that leaned into the wind. Leona drove with one hand over the top of the wheel, the other tapping the door in a quiet, restless rhythm.

They turned onto a dirt lane rutted by years of runoff. The trailer at the end was small, the siding pitted and faded. But the porch was swept, and a potted plant leaned stubbornly into the sun.

Dan glanced toward the trailers. "Seems like a tough place to grow up."

Leona didn't respond right away.

"I called her mom yesterday," she said. "To let her know we'd be gone most of the day. Maybe overnight."

Dan glanced over. "How'd that go?"

Leona gave a thin smile. "She said I could take her. Something along the lines of, 'Fine by me. Just don't go filling her head with your crap and have her back by tomorrow.' Vintage Candace Bright."

Dan blinked. "Star's mom is Candace Bright?"

Leona nodded. "Yeah. You know her?"

"I think so," he said. "There was a group of locals drinking at one of the overlooks, drifting toward trouble. She didn't say much, but she was with a rough crowd."

Leona gave a short breath. "That's Candace. Worn to the bone but still standing."

Leona slowed as they approached the last trailer in the row. There was a stack of bottled water near the steps and laundry clipped to a rope strung between the porch post and a sapling. The siding faded to a soft gray, tin skirting bowed in one spot like it had been kicked in years ago.

Dan caught movement behind one of the small windows, a shadow shifting, then a face. A woman's, framed by dull glass. She didn't come out. Just watched.

Candace Bright.

Leona didn't acknowledge her. She just cut the engine and waited.

The door creaked open, and Star stepped out.

Her hair was tied back with a faded bandana, backpack slung over one shoulder. She moved with a quiet purpose, but there was something bright behind her eyes. Not wide-eyed excitement. A low, steady flame.

Before she reached the truck, Shankley jumped down, tail already wagging.

Star froze. Just for a second.

Then she crouched.

"Hey," she said softly. "Hey, you."

Shankley approached slowly, then quicker, nose bumping against her hands, body wiggling in that loose, happy way dogs reserve for people who feel right.

Star smiled, open and unguarded, and rubbed behind his ears like they'd known each other for years.

Dan watched from the passenger seat. "Well," he murmured, "that didn't take long."

Leona smiled too, but hers was quieter. She stepped out and opened the rear door.

"You ready?" she asked.

Star stood, her hand still resting on Shankley's back.

"Yeah," she said. "I packed last night."

There was no goodbye from the window. Just the faint sense of eyes behind the glass as they pulled away.

They were on the highway now, heading north on 89. Open land rolled out in soft folds—summer, warm and dry—mountains rising farther off.

Star sat in the back, one leg tucked under her, backpack at her feet. Shankley lay stretched across the seat beside her, his head resting on her thigh, breathing slow and content. She rested a hand on his back, her gaze flicking between the window and the front seats.

Dan leaned his elbow on the door, fingers tapping the glass. "So," he said, "tell us about this mentor of yours."

Leona didn't answer right away. She adjusted her hand on the wheel, eyes on the road.

"Martha," she said at last. "She taught anthropology at the university for a while. But her classroom was always bigger than that. I knew her before the degrees. Before the conferences."

Dan glanced over. "She's from the reservation?"

Leona nodded. "She was always there. One of those people who doesn't stand out unless you're paying attention. But if you did—you wouldn't forget her."

"Was she a teacher there too?"

"A kind of keeper," Leona said. "Of stories. Of time. Of the in-between things people overlook."

Star looked up from the dog. "Did she help you leave?"

Leona was quiet for a moment. "She didn't push me," she said. "Didn't tell me I had to get out to be anything. Just made sure I understood that leaving didn't mean forgetting. That there was power in both staying and going, so long as you knew why you were doing either."

Dan looked out the window. Farms and towns passed in a soft blur.

"Does she still teach?" he asked.

"Not in a classroom," Leona said. "But people still find their way to her."

Star shifted again, her hand resting on Shankley's side.

"Do you think she'll like me?" she asked.

Leona didn't glance back. Just kept her voice steady. "Martha doesn't worry about liking people. She listens. And she sees."

Bozeman came into view—gridded streets, the sharp clean lines of new buildings pressing up against older ones with peeling paint and softened corners. The car turned down a residential side street not far from the university campus. Bicycles leaned against porch railings. A couple of students kicked a soccer ball barefoot in the patchy grass of a nearby lawn.

Leona slowed in front of a small blue house with a rust-colored door and a wraparound porch. Wind chimes clinked beneath the eaves and a carved wooden bear sat by the steps.

"This is her place," Leona said, shifting into park.

Dan took it in. The house wasn't large, but it had a lived-in order disguised as clutter.

Shankley lifted his head from Star's lap. She sat straight, eyes drawn to the house's cluttered charm, the color and warmth of it.

Leona turned in her seat. "She probably already knows we're here."

On cue, the front door opened.

Martha stood in the doorway, hand resting on the frame. She was in her sixties, or older, with silver-streaked hair braided down one side, and a faded university sweatshirt over a long denim skirt.

Her eyes lit up when she saw Leona.

"Han Leona, there you are," she said, voice warm with welcome.

Leona stepped out of the car and walked up the path.

"Han Martha, I brought the company we spoke of," she called, a note of affection in her voice.

"I figured," Martha said. "The wind told me someone new was coming."

Dan opened his door and Star followed—slower, hands in her jacket pockets.

Shankley leapt out and gave himself a brisk shake, before trotting up alongside them.

Martha's eyes landed on Star.

"You're the one with sharp questions," she said. "Good. Questions keep us from getting too proud."

Then she looked at Dan. Pausing as she took in the whole of him.

"You carry something heavy."

Dan's mouth opened slightly, but no words came.

Martha nodded, just once, like that was enough for now.

"Well," she said, stepping aside. "Come in. The kettle's on."

The house smelled of cedar and something warm rising from the kitchen like it had been on low for hours. Sun filtered through gauze curtains, softened the light inside the house. The walls were lined with books—stacks leaned into corners, bookmarks peeking like soft tongues. A few shelves held small carved figures, three river stones stacked one atop the other.

Martha led them in without ceremony. She didn't ask if they wanted tea, she simply poured it, a quiet act of hospitality. She used clay mugs without handles. The kind that needed both hands.

"Sit where you feel comfortable," she said, her voice soft but edged with expectation.

Dan stood before choosing a low chair near the window. Star hovered, her eyes taking in the space noticing the objects, the heavy woven blanket folded at the back of the couch. She sat cross-legged on the rug, her back straight, hands in her lap.

Martha set a mug on the floor beside her, then turned to Dan with another.

"You came burdened," she said. "That's all right."

Dan didn't answer, just nodded, eyes lowered to the rising steam.

Leona took a seat near the hearth, a straight-backed wooden chair worn smooth at the arms.

Martha lowered herself onto a cushion opposite Star. Her brow was smooth but around her eyes were years of crinkles.

"You pay attention," she said to Star. "That's good. But you don't give much away."

Star met her gaze. Steady.

"I watch," she said.

Martha nodded. "Watching is learning. As long as you don't forget to speak when the time comes."

Outside, a breeze shifted the wind chimes under the eaves. A dog barked as a truck rumbled down the street.

Martha turned back toward the center of the room. Her voice was calm, unhurried.

"Well," she said. "Tell me why you're really here."

Star looked down at her mug. She hadn't touched the tea yet.

"I didn't ask to come," she said, not defensive, just honest.

Martha nodded. "But still, you came."

Star glanced toward the photos on the wall. "I didn't know what it was supposed to be."

"Sometimes it's better that way," Martha said. "No fixed shape means there's room to move around inside it."

Star's hand rested against the side of the mug. Her thumb traced the rim once, then settled.

"People talk," she said. "About me and about my mom. Like I'm a version of her they're waiting to see happen."

Leona stayed still in her chair. Dan did too.

Martha didn't react. "Does that happen a lot?"

Star nodded once. "They say it like it's already decided. Like I won't have a say in it."

Martha sipped her tea, then set it down on a woven coaster. "People like to repeat what they've seen. That doesn't make it a prophecy."

Star held Martha's gaze.

"Sounds as though your mom's had to carry more than her share," Martha said, her voice even. "Some of it spilled, but that doesn't make cleaning it your responsibility."

Star finally took a sip. The warmth hit her mouth like something unexpected. She didn't speak again, but her shoulders loosened a little.

Martha watched her without crowding.

"You get to choose what you hold onto," she said. "And when."

Leona leaned back in her chair, her hands wrapped around her tea. She hadn't spoken since they arrived.

She looked toward Martha, then to Star, and finally let her gaze rest on Dan.

"Dan came up from Colorado," she said, voice steady. "He's a wildlife officer. He knew the backcountry better than most and worked alone a lot."

Dan shifted uncomfortably in his seat but said nothing.

Leona continued. "He's not here, in Montana, because of a job though. Not really."

Martha raised an eyebrow, faint amusement in the lines of her face.

"I've seen how he moves through the park. How he sees things."

She let that hang a moment.

"It's not just tracks and scat with him," she said. "It runs deeper."

Dan didn't look up, but his jaw flexed once. Star glanced toward him, curious.

Leona's tone didn't soften, if anything, it grew more matter of fact.

"I don't know what you'd call it," she said. "But I've felt it. He's close to the land. Maybe too close, sometimes."

Now she looked at Martha. "I brought him because I thought you might know what to do with that."

Martha nodded once, a nod that carried weight without needing to explain itself.

She looked at Dan, calm as she considered.

"You see things others don't," she said.

Dan finally met her gaze.

"Maybe. I didn't ask for it."

"No one does," Martha replied. "But you can still choose what you do with it."

Dan's eyes lingered on the rim of his mug, the faint chip in the glaze. He'd been holding it in both hands but now placed the cup on the floor.

"I spent years thinking I understood the job," he said, finally. His voice was low. "Track the animals. Keep the people in line. Do your part to hold the boundary."

He paused. No one filled the space.

"But the line kept moving. I'd think I had it—what was natural, what was right—and then something would change. The animals would tell me first. Just not in ways I could explain."

Martha watched him.

Dan took a breath that didn't quite make it all the way in.

"I started to feel like maybe the problem wasn't out there."

Another pause. Then, almost an afterthought:

"Maybe it was me."

Star looked at him, then away, instinctively giving him space.

Leona didn't move.

Martha let it sit a moment longer.

"Grief can wear a lot of coats."

Dan's brow furrowed and his hands came to his face as he rubbed his eyes.

At last, Leona leaned forward slightly.

"I heard from Clara last week," she said, breaking the spell. "She's still up on Standing Rock, helping with the garden project."

Martha's face brightened just a little. "That girl always had good soil in her."

"She said they're starting early this year. Already got spinach coming up."

Martha nodded, clearly pleased.

"They got the irrigation sorted?"

"Mostly," Leona said. "Still leaky as all get, but they got a donated tank—rigged a patchwork fix, and Clara says the kids love it. They've started naming the plants."

Star smiled at that.

Leona looked toward her. "Clara used to sit behind me in history class. She never said a word. Then one day we both got in trouble for correcting the teacher during the Columbus unit."

Dan raised an eyebrow.

"She didn't say anything then either," Leona said. "Just slid her desk forward so we could serve detention next to each other."

Even Martha laughed at that.

The room eased, just a little.

The light through the windows had softened, brushing everything in a low amber hue, the feel it sometimes gets near the end of the day.

Martha rose and moved to the side table by the kitchen. She returned holding a small box made of dark wood, worn smooth at the edges.

"I've got some work that needs doing over the break," she said, looking at Star. "Sorting field notes, scanning old records. It's nothing fancy, but I could use a hand, if you're open to it."

Star blinked. She didn't smile, exactly, but her face lifted a little. "Yeah," she said. "I'd like that."

Martha nodded. "Good."

She looked to Dan and Leona.

"There's a cabin. It belongs to a friend, a professor who spends most of the year out of the country. It's quiet with no cell service. Plenty of trees. He lets me offer it when I think someone might need it."

Dan looked at her, something unreadable in his expression.

"You're offering us a vacation?"

"I'm offering you stillness," she said.

Leona didn't answer right away, but Dan saw the moment she accepted. Just a shift in her posture. A softening at the jaw.

"Late summer," Martha added. "Before school starts up again. If you want it, I'll hold the key."

No one said thank you. It didn't need saying.

They stayed a while longer, talking about nothing—dogs and books. Star eventually reached for her tea again. Dan gave Shankley a piece of dried apple from his pack.

When they finally stood to leave, Martha didn't walk them out. She simply stood at the door, one hand resting lightly on the frame.

As they stepped onto the porch, she spoke. "We're all carrying something. That's normal."

Dan turned his head as she continued.

"Just don't forget to set it down once in a while. Even stones need sunlight."

TWENTY-FIVE

THE TRAIL CLIMBED SLOWLY, tracing the edge of a ridgeline above Lamar Valley. The grasses down below were gold in the heat, rippling with wind. In the woods, the earth was dry and sweet-smelling, sun on pine needles. Flies buzzed lazily in the pockets of still air.

Dan moved easily, the rhythm of the hike, Leona kept pace beside him—her gaze more often in the trees than on the trail.

They'd been walking for hours.

"Do you ever think about how trees talk to each other?" she asked.

Dan looked over, squinting against the light. "Like—in a forest wisdom kind of way?"

She half-smiled. "In a real way. Through their roots. Fungal threads connect them and carry messages. Chemicals, electrical signals. If one tree's under threat, the others know and they adjust."

Dan gave a small nod. "I think I read something about that once. I thought it sounded like good PR for trees."

Leona chuckled. "It's more than PR. It's memory. They look like individuals, but they're not. They're a community."

They kept walking. The trail narrowed, winding through a denser patch of lodgepole and aspen. Shadows moved between the trees, the slow breathing of the forest.

"You focus on animals," Leona said. "Tracks. Movement. The loud parts of nature."

Dan ducked under a low branch, felt the bark scrape the back of his shoulder.

"I guess I notice what moves," he said.

"You don't have to name it," Leona said. "Just remember, other stuff—plants, insects. They're part of it too."

Dan glanced at her, but she wasn't looking at him. She was watching a flicker hopping along a sun-bleached branch, its head cocked as it worked loose a bit of bark.

The wind shifted.

There was a smell, faint but distinct, distant soil.

Dan paused. His breath caught, not from exertion, but from something else. Like a presence under the surface of things.

And then he heard a sound, far off sound and stretched thin by distance.

Not a growl. Not a cry.

A single howl, long and low.

They reached a crest where the trees thinned and the view opened. They were through the park, the boundary behind them, though there were no signs—just a subtle shift in the way the trail looked like it had been walked a little less.

Leona paused, took a long drink from her bottle. "Outside the park. The land's still wild. But the rules get loose."

Dan scanned the terrain ahead, there weren't any trails, but an old game path drifted off into a cluster of fir and dogwood down the slope.

"You see that?" he said, nodding toward it. "Something's moved through."

Leona followed his gaze. "Do you think it's fresh?"

Dan stepped off the trail, already descending. "Only one way to find out."

They moved in silence for a few minutes, stepping over twisted roots and dry logs. The forest here was tighter, branches low, thick with lichen, the light cooler and green-edged.

Dan crouched, brushing his fingers along a faint depression in the soil. "It was big. Could be a wolf."

Leona was scanning farther down the slope. She froze, one hand raised slightly.

He followed her line of sight.

Just beyond the clearing, a figure crouched low behind a stump in full camouflage. A rifle leaned nearby, resting against a deadfall. The man was working carefully at something on the ground, his hands moving with practiced efficiency.

Dan's jaw tightened as he recognized the shape of the snare.

He dropped beside Leona without a word.

She didn't look at him, just whispered, "You want to see what he does."

Dan nodded, breathing slowly but sharp-edged. The heat was already rising in his chest.

They watched.

The poacher finished adjusting the snare, then lit a cigarette like he owned the land. He didn't glance around. Didn't hurry.

Dan shifted. His breath had shortened.

"This isn't hunting," he muttered. "This is just—lazy cruelty."

Leona turned slightly toward him, eyes flicking up. What passed between them wasn't judgment.

Recognition.

Dan exhaled hard.

Then he stood.

The movement was sudden. Leona didn't stop him.

"Hey!" Dan's voice cut across the clearing. Sharp. Controlled, but only just.

The man flinched, spun. His hand twitched toward the rifle.

"Don't," Dan warned. "Step away from the trap. Now."

The man froze. His eyes narrowed.

"Who the hell—?"

"Wildlife officer." Dan held up his badge but didn't lower his stance. "This area's under active protection. That snare's illegal."

The man hesitated, eyes flicking from Dan to the trap.

Dan took a slow step forward. "I said move away."

The poacher cursed under his breath but backed off, boots crunching in the underbrush.

Dan approached with deliberate steps. He disarmed the snare, coiled the wire, and picked up the bait sack with a look of pure disgust.

"You come out here again with this kind of setup," he said, "and you won't be walking away with just a warning."

The man didn't respond. Just spat to the side and trudged off, muttering.

Dan didn't look back until he was gone.

Leona stepped up beside him. Quiet and steady.

Dan stared at the trap in his hand. The twisted wire looked smaller now, but somehow heavier.

"It's like they don't see anything alive in what's left out here," he said.

"They don't know how to look," Leona replied.

Dan nodded slowly. "I'm not sure I can keep doing this."

Her voice was low. "Then don't do it alone."

They walked back to the trail in silence.

The path sloped gently through a narrow stretch of pine, the light growing long and golden behind them. A thrush darted through the branches overhead, but otherwise the woods felt still.

Dan carried the snare in one hand, the metal loose in his grip. His mouth was tight, his jaw set. He hadn't spoken since they'd left the clearing.

Leona walked beside him, matching his pace without comment.

After a while, she said, "He wasn't scared of us."

Dan's voice came low. "He should've been."

They walked on.

"He lit a cigarette," Dan added. "Set a trap for a wolf and lit a cigarette like it was just another day."

The anger in his voice was there, but dulled, rounded off by something heavier.

He stopped at a bend where the trail narrowed. Looked down at the wire in his hand.

"I don't know what to do with this," he said, not raising his voice. Not asking a question.

Leona didn't answer. She just stood with him.

The forest stretched quietly around them.

They stepped over a fallen branch, then around a boulder furred with moss. A small clearing opened to the left, a pocket of flattened grass where something had bedded down.

Dan paused.

Not for a reason. Not consciously.

He just stopped.

Leona kept walking a few steps, then glanced back. "What's up, are you okay?"

Dan nodded. But he wasn't looking at her.

His eyes had gone to the tree line, where the shadows ran deeper, and something in the air felt denser.

Leona waited. But Dan didn't move.

The warmth of the day clung to the rocks, but Dan caught something beneath it. A pressure—not on his body, but within it. Like a memory surfacing that didn't belong to him.

The sounds around him sharpened.

A pinecone cracking under something small.

The faint trace of musk—not human, not prey.

The earth seemed to rise beneath him. The scent of fur.

Of blood.

Of cool streambeds and warm breath in the dark.

And the forest was no longer *around* him.

It was *in* him.

He heard something—distant. A second howl. Not loud or long.

But this time, he felt closer to it.

Leona said something, soft and concerned, but it barely reached him.

The light changed and his chest tightened with urgency. His vision blurred then sharpened again.

And something else stepped forward.

The world snapped into scent.

The earth told a story through what remained.

And the wolf moved.

With rhythm—and without caution.

The body was made to run—to *trot*, endlessly, tirelessly. Across ridges. Through drainages. The pads of its feet barely touched the earth before lifting again.

The trail was a path of decisions made by scent and wind.

Somewhere out there was the pack.

He felt a blood-deep certainty that he was not alone. That others moved too, felt this wind, knew this pace.

The wolf turned, he'd sensed a trace. Faint and warm. Blood beneath fur.

It moved without thought.

A squirrel—lean, mountain-bred, wary and wild.

The wolf surged forward. A clean snap of brush. A twist of muscle. A final leap.

Teeth closed.

The wolf held it, panting lightly through its nose. Blood slicked the fur. Warmth. Life passing into life.

When the wolf finished, it licked its muzzle once and moved on.

The sun had lowered, stretching long bands of shadow between the trees. The air cooled, not sharply, but enough to change the sounds—fewer insects, a different weight to the wind.

A rise in the land led to a narrow stream, choked with reeds and ringed by willow. The wolf lowered its head to drink, tongue flicking with rhythm and ease. The water was cold and tasted of stones and slow melt.

There was no sound of other wolves. No scent strong enough to trace.

The scent of the squirrel was gone. The stream, too.

Its legs felt longer now, not stronger.

It took another step and stumbled, catching itself with a short growl.

The world was dimming. Not just from dusk.

From *separation*.

It stopped.

And for the first time something *resisted*.

The wind brushed along its flank, but it didn't feel like before. The pelt—*skin*—felt unfamiliar. Heavy in a new way.

The eyes still saw clearly—movement, texture, distance. But meaning had started to slip back in. *Names* began to return.

Tree.

Snare.

Leona.

The wolf blinked.

Not because it needed to. But because something *in* it had asked.

The air carried scent—but with it came memory—bait, cigarette.

He didn't want to return.

This had felt right. Clean. Real. His body had purpose, his mind hadn't ached.

Grief hadn't followed.

But already it was slipping.

The body *shivered*.

A sound moved through the trees.

A voice.

Low. Even.

"Dan."

His body flinched. Just slightly.

Ears turned. The muscles tensed, uncertain whether to run or listen.

"Dan," —closer now, but still soft.

The wolf stepped back, half a pace. One foot landed wrong—heel-first.

Human.

The forest was still there. Still open, still waiting.

But now the name had weight.

That name held everything—doubt, grief, that coiled wire still sitting in his hand.

And the woman whose voice didn't chase him.

Who waited.

The forest was dim now, the shadows softening at the edges. Time had loosened. The smell of soil, warm, dry, and familiar, held steady in his nose.

A hand pressed into the dirt. Shaking from the strain of being pulled apart and slowly resewn.

His heartbeat slowed.

The world no longer sang like it had. But the memory of it remained.

Somewhere nearby, Leona waited.

No voice.

Only presence.

He closed his eyes.

Just to listen.

Twenty-six

He woke with a start, breath caught in his throat.

The world came back, too bright and too dull all at once. Light speared through the trees and flashed hard against his eyes. The air smelled of sweat and skin. It was too dry, too human.

Dan blinked hard. His limbs felt wrong—too long, too slow, too separate. His fingers twitched against the forest floor, struggling to recall their purpose.

Leaves rustled nearby and a shape moved.

"Dan?"

The voice cut through like a clean line in fog.

Leona.

He turned toward the sound, but it took effort, his head was heavy, his eyes swimming.

She crouched a few feet away, arms resting on her knees. Calm, but wary. Watching him as if he might still be something else.

"You were gone a long time. Hours," she said. "Your body didn't move. Not once."

Dan's throat was dry. "I was gone?" he rasped.

He tried to sit up. The movement cost him. Every part of him resisted, as though his body had been borrowed by someone else. He braced on his palms and looked at his hands—his knuckles were scarred, dirt under the nails.

"I heard them," he whispered. "I was *with* them."

Leona's expression didn't change, but he saw something flicker behind her eyes. Concern, maybe. Or recognition.

"I could smell it all—distance, presence, absence. It was beautiful. Like being lit from the inside. I didn't want it to end."

Leona looked away, her gaze following something invisible through the trees. Her arms folded—holding something in. When she finally spoke, her voice was quieter.

"I don't know exactly what this does to a person," she said. "But we have stories."

Dan watched her.

She turned back to him. "I think the longer you're out there—the harder it gets to come back. Not physically. But on the inside."

She touched him now, for the first time.

"I'm not saying that's wrong," Leona added. "Animals know things we've forgotten. Maybe you're remembering something we lost."

Dan's throat tightened. "I didn't want to come back."

"I know."

But there was no judgment in it. Just sadness.

She crouched beside him, close but not touching this time. "Whatever this is—you don't have to face it alone."

Dan held her gaze and, tentatively, he reached for her hand.

* * *

Leona drove them back toward Mammoth. Slowly, like there was no rush to get back to things the way they used to be.

"What happened to you," she said eventually. "It's like you disappeared."

He looked out the window. "It felt like days."

Leona kept her eyes on the road. "I don't know what happens if you stay away too long. But I wonder—if the thread between the body and the rest of you just—"

They pulled up to his unit just as the last of the sun slipped behind the ridge. The shadows stretched long across the gravel lot. Shankley was waiting behind the front door, his tail up, ears alert.

Dan opened the door slowly and stepped in. His legs were steadier now.

Shankley barked once, a soft yap more than anything, then approached, but stopped short. He sniffed the air, ears tilting back slightly. Dan knelt and held out a hand.

"Hey, buddy."

But Shankley didn't move forward. Instead, he circled wide and went straight to Leona, pressing his side gently against her leg.

She reached down and gave his flank a rub. "It's okay," she murmured. "He's still in there."

Dan stayed crouched for a moment, watching them.

Leona paused in the doorway. Her eyes searched his face—reading something she couldn't quite name.

"I don't know if you can choose when you go," she said softly. "Or if it's something deeper than choice. But if there's any part of you that decides—"

She hesitated.

"Try to hold on. Stay here, when you can. You matter in this world too."

Dan forced himself to meet her gaze. "I'll try."

Leona held the look, then turned and stepped off the porch, her figure fading into the twilight.

He stood in the doorway, unmoving. Shankley lingered just inside, ears pinned slightly, head tilted—not approaching, not retreating.

Dan crouched low and waited. After a moment, the dog gave a soft whine and took a cautious step closer.

The door swung closed behind them with a soft *click*, leaving the night outside.

TWENTY-SEVEN

MARTHA OPENED THE DOOR before they knocked.

"Good timing," she said. "My door's always open to you two."

She stepped back to let them in. Dan followed Leona inside, nodding a quiet hello. The house was much as he remembered it, light filtering through small windows—clutter that belonged.

"How was the drive?" Martha asked.

"Not too bad," Leona said. "The roads were clear."

Martha moved to the counter and picked up a folded index card. "Here's directions, there's a turnoff, just past mile marker sixteen. Look for the fence with the broken top rail. It's easy to miss."

Leona took the card and glanced at the simple sketch. "Got it."

"There's no cell service up there," Martha added. "There's a fire laid in the woodstove, and there's more wood stacked outside, and I left matches in the top drawer."

She turned to Dan. Her smile softened, but it didn't quite reach her eyes.

Dan met her gaze but said nothing.

She stepped forward and placed her hand gently on his arm. "Remember to stay where your feet are," she said. "The rest of you will catch up."

Dan gave a small nod, unsure whether it helped or unsettled him more.

"I'll get the truck started," he said, and stepped outside.

The door clicked shut behind him.

Martha waited before speaking.

"He's changed," she said.

Leona didn't argue. "I know."

Martha's voice dropped. "The spirit isn't something you can leash."

* * *

They pulled off the road where the dirt lot opened beneath a stand of spruce. No sign, just a gap in the trees and the faintest impression of a trail.

Dan turned off the engine. Neither of them moved for a moment.

Dan opened his door and stepped out. The air was cooler here, thin and dry, with that clean high-altitude quiet that made every sound feel sharper. Shankley jumped down after him, gave a soft shake, then stood still, nose lifted.

Leona handed Dan a pack from the back seat. "Will you take that one?"

He nodded.

They started up the trail, the forest rising slowly around them. The path was narrow but well-worn, scattered with pine needles and the occasional patch of damp earth tucked in the shade. The only sound was their boots and the quick rhythm of steady breathing.

Half a mile passed easily.

When they crested the final rise, the cabin came into view, a small structure tucked into a bowl of trees, roof dark with weather, chimney leaning slightly. The windows reflected the sky.

Dan stopped just shy of the clearing. Shankley padded forward, circled the porch once, then sat.

Leona gave a small nod. "Here we are."

Dan stepped up onto the porch and pulled the key from his jacket pocket. The lock turned stiffly—unused but not stuck. He pushed the door open with the side of his hand.

It creaked but didn't resist. Inside, the light was dim but clean. Wood walls. The room was square and uncluttered with a table, two chairs, and a small wood stove in the corner. There was a narrow counter with a basin and a dented kettle on the counter.

Leona stepped in behind him, setting her pack down near the door. She didn't say anything, just looked around, taking it in.

Dan crossed to the far wall and opened the single interior door.

Two narrow beds, parallel with space between. Thin wool blankets folded neatly.

He returned to the main room and crouched beside the stove. The firebox was clean, kindling stacked inside, just as Martha had said.

Leona opened a drawer in the corner cabinet. "Matches," she said. Then lifted something else. "Oh, and a deck of cards."

Dan half-smiled. "In case of long evenings."

She placed them on the table. "This would be a pretty great place for some long evenings."

He moved to the window. It looked north, toward a peak that still held snow in deep shaded pockets.

The trees were close but didn't smother the cabin. It was quiet in that way only deep country can be—no hum, no static.

Shankley settled on the floor with a heavy sigh.

They were out of reach.

After dropping their packs and letting Shankley drink from the tin bowl by the door, they stepped back out, walking slowly into the trees behind the cabin. A faint trail, soft ground and the weave of roots beneath the needles.

Late afternoon light tinged gold.

Dan kept his eyes low, scanning for deadfall—dry limbs, bark flaking, light enough to burn clean. He gathered a few and passed them to Leona, who carried them against her hip.

This wasn't dramatic like Yellowstone. No soaring cliffs or rushing water. Just a slope of spruce and fir, a few aspens, green leaves quaking gently.

Dan felt the connection.

At one point, Leona paused and looked up through the trees. Her hand brushed the bark beside her.

"They remember," she said softly.

Dan didn't ask what she meant. He understood, in some way he couldn't explain.

They carried the branches back in silence.

Back at the cabin, they worked without much talk.

Leona unpacked a small sack of groceries—two sweet potatoes, a bag of rice, an onion, a can of black beans, a little jar of salt. She sat them on the table and gave Dan a glance that wasn't quite a question.

He peeled the potatoes with his pocketknife while she lit the stove. The flame clicked once, then caught with a low hiss. The kettle went on for tea, the pot for rice beside it. The cutting board was a slab of wood that had been cut from the forest.

Dan chopped the onion while Leona rinsed beans in the tin colander. She moved with a kind of practiced calm, not hurried, not distracted. They passed things back and forth without direction. The salt. A pan to roast the potatoes in.

As the food warmed the aroma filled the room—earthy, familiar, unremarkable in the best way.

"You've done this before," Leona said.

Dan gave a small shrug. "I like simple food."

She nodded. "Simple's honest."

When the food was ready, they sat at the table and ate slowly, watching the last light through the window as it touched the treetops.

The fire crackled softly in the stove.

Leona added one of the thinner logs they'd gathered earlier, nudging it into place with the iron poker. The flame caught to life and the cabin warmed, first the air, then the floor beneath their feet.

Dan sat at the edge of his chair, elbows on his knees, holding the last of his tea. He wasn't looking at Leona, just watching the way the firelight flickered on the wall.

"I didn't tell you everything," he said.

She didn't ask what he meant.

"About the wolf," he went on. "It wasn't like the time with the crow or even the otter. I wasn't just inside it. I *was* it. I didn't feel like I had left anything behind. Not even me."

He looked up. Leona's face was calm, but there was something behind her eyes. Listening closely.

"I could feel them," he said. "The pack. Not with words or thoughts. Just—being. Motion. Purpose. Like I belonged, without having to earn it."

A long breath left him.

"I didn't want to come back."

The fire snapped once, a sudden pop of sap.

Leona sat across from him, hands resting in her lap. She spoke carefully.

"I felt it. When you came back." She paused. "Something about you had... stayed out there."

Dan nodded once, slowly.

"I don't know what that means," he said. "If it's over. Or just beginning."

Leona didn't speak right away. Then, gently:

"I think the world lets you go more easily than you think. Especially when you start wanting it."

Dan looked at her.

"And do you think that's wrong?"

She shook her head. "I think it's dangerous. Not because you're drawn to the wild. But because the rest of us might not follow."

The fire shifted again, collapsing inward as one log burned through. Outside, the trees moved in wind they couldn't hear.

Dan leaned back in his chair and closed his eyes for a moment.

Leona watched the flame through the stove's small glass pane, as if something inside it might explain what words couldn't.

She moved forward, elbows on her knees, hands loosely clasped. The fire cast her face in shifting light—half in glow, half in shadow.

"When I was younger," she said, "I thought the old ways were perfect. Like we had it right until the white world ruined everything."

She gave a small shake of her head. "That's not true. Our people fought each other. Burned villages. The cliff dwellings in the Southwest weren't built for the view. They were built to hide. To survive."

Dan stayed quiet.

"We lived close to the land, yes. But it wasn't some peaceful dream. It was full of fear, too. But it was *connected.* When the bison were taken, when the children were sent away, when the land was carved up and fenced—we didn't just lose comfort. We lost the rhythm of who we were."

Her voice didn't rise. If anything, it softened.

"But even after all that—we're still here. Still learning and still listening."

She looked over at him now.

"I don't believe humans are separate from nature. I do think we forgot. I don't believe how we live now is permanent. How can it be? It's out of balance. Nature doesn't let that stand."

She leaned back, exhaled slowly.

"Whether it's fire or frost or something slower—balance will come. Maybe we go too. Maybe we don't. But the world—the real world, it doesn't go anywhere."

The fire popped softly.

"We're not the first to think we're in control."

Dan didn't respond right away. He sat still, hands folded loosely between his knees, eyes fixed on a knot in the floorboards.

Shankley stirred in his sleep and let out a yip like he was chasing something.

Dan shifted slightly, elbows on his knees again. When he spoke, his voice was low.

"I get what you're saying," he said. "I do."

He paused, then looked at her.

"Animals understand," he spoke carefully. "They know about plague and what it can do, not as a word but as a feeling deep inside."

Leona's gaze held steady, but she didn't interrupt.

"It's not about death. It's about the shrinking of space. The way you're always alert because there's always something coming. A trap or a bullet. A car that doesn't stop."

He leaned back, exhaled.

"Humanity has pushed it out of balance.

"Seven, eight billion people clawing at what's left of the world to keep some version of comfort alive. That's not forgetting."

His jaw tightened, just a little.

"We're not part of nature anymore. We peeled ourselves away. Broke from it."

He looked at the fire now, not her.

"I don't think we'll fix that. I think it's already ruined. And maybe that's what it takes. A reckoning. The world will go on. But I'm not sure we do."

The fire had burned low, casting the walls in a soft, uneven glow. Dan added one last piece of wood, not to chase off the cold, but to keep the silence company.

Leona stood and carried their bowls to the counter, rinsing them in the basin with a little water from the kettle. Dan folded the blankets on the couch and moved to the bedroom.

The two beds were simple. Narrow. Quiet in their own corners.

He sat on the edge of one and pulled off his boots. Shankley curled up on the floor between them without hesitation, already half-asleep. The air in the room was warmer now but still edged with mountain cold.

Leona came in a few minutes later, hair unbraided, face calm but unreadable. She turned down the blanket on the other bed, then paused.

The light from the fire in the main room flickered against the doorway. Outside, the wind had stilled.

She crossed the floor slowly and slipped into Dan's bed without a word.

Her hand found his beneath the blanket, their fingers intertwining.

He let out a breath and pulled her close.

* * *

Dan woke to the faint sound of water slipping from the eaves.

He lay still for a moment, listening. The roof creaked softly, settling. Outside, the air was brighter, sharper. He rose carefully, pulling on his boots and coat. Leona stirred slightly but didn't wake. Shankley rose without a sound and followed him to the door.

When Dan stepped outside, the light caught him.

A shower had passed in the night. The trees were beaded with droplets, dark with moisture. On the distant peak, a clean white dusting traced the ridgeline. The sky was clear, pale and wide, as though it had been wiped clean.

He stepped down into the wet earth and walked with Shankley through the edge of the trees, the dog padding quietly beside him.

Behind him, the cabin door creaked gently.

Leona stepped out, jacket over her shoulders, hair pulled back roughly. She didn't say anything. Just joined him, the soft sound of her boots moving through damp ground.

They stood side by side, looking out toward the distant white peak. Dan reached for her hand without looking, and she gave it to him without hesitation.

They stayed three nights.
The days moved slowly, but well.

Twenty-Eight

The park had the feel of late summer—everything dry and overused. Grasses brittle at the edges, dust rising from the trails. The bison didn't seem to mind. They lounged where they pleased.

Dan leaned against the hood of the truck. Below, a bull bison dozed in the sun, indifferent to the tourists who watched from the turnout.

Wyatt stood beside him, arms crossed, scanning the crowd. "Do you ever think how strange this must look to them?" he said.

Dan followed his gaze. "To the bison?"

Wyatt nodded. "Yeah, the whole crowd staring, snapping pictures. Like they're in a zoo but maybe we're the ones behind the fences."

Dan gave a dry half-smile. "I don't think they care. They've seen worse."

"True," Wyatt said, exhaling slowly. "Still. It's a hell of a thing."

The sun was high; sunlight filtered through the haze of distant fires. The wind moved in low passes across the basin, lifting little swirls of dust from the road's edge. Shankley lay in the shade of the truck's back tire.

After a while, Wyatt said, "I think we should head up toward Trail Creek? I heard there's been some fence trouble but it's probably nothing."

Dan capped the thermos and slid it back behind the seat. "Yeah," he said. "Let's go."

They pulled back onto the main road, tires humming low over the cracked asphalt. The truck climbed slowly through open country, the sagebrush giving way to stands of lodgepole and scattered fir. In the far distance, the haze thickened, a smudge of smoke somewhere west, too far to smell but close enough to tint the light.

Wyatt adjusted the air vent with one hand, the other resting on the wheel. "Smoke's showing up earlier every year," he said.

Dan didn't respond at first. His eyes were on the ridgeline, where the haze bled into the sky. "Not early," he said finally. "Just normal now."

They passed tourists pulled over at a blind curve, doors flung open, someone trying to photograph an elk from twenty feet away.

Wyatt gave a half-laugh. "The elk are gonna unionize."

Dan didn't smile this time. He was watching the slope. "That one's limping," he said.

Wyatt glanced over. "Yeah. Back leg. Probably clipped on the highway last week. You want to check it?"

Dan shook his head. "Let it be for now. It's still moving."

The truck climbed higher, the road narrowing and the fences beginning to appear again, lines in the dirt, rusted wire strung between leaning posts. Out here, public and private blurred. Ranchland, tight up against the edge of the park.

The radio crackled to life.

"Dispatch to Unit Four."

Wyatt picked it up. "Go ahead."

"I've got a rancher out near Trail Creek reporting a dead bison just inside his fenceline. Says he fired in self-defense and he sounds heated."

Wyatt looked over at Dan, his expression unreadable.

"Copy that," he said. "We're ten minutes out."

He set the radio back in its cradle.

Dan was still looking out the window, his jaw tight.

Wyatt gave it a moment, then asked, lightly, "Do you want to take the lead on this one?"

Dan didn't turn. Just said, "Sure."

The road narrowed as they climbed toward the ranch. Fencing appeared in irregular runs, some of it upright, some slumped, and patched with baling wire and old rails. A rusted stock gate leaned open where the gravel widened into a turnout.

Wyatt slowed as they passed under a faded metal sign with no name, just a cattle brand welded into a flat sheet. Beyond it, the land opened into rough pasture, dry and yellowing. A battered pickup was parked near the tree line, the hood dusted and rifle racked behind the rear glass.

The bison lay maybe thirty yards out from the fence, half in shadow.

Wyatt parked but left the engine running for a moment. "Ready?" he asked, glancing across the cab.

Dan opened the door without answering.

The rancher stood at the edge of the field, arms folded, the kind of posture that said he was already done explaining.

"Glad someone finally showed," he called. "Been waiting for you guys to show up."

Wyatt kept his tone easy. "We appreciate it."

The man gave a curt nod, then gestured toward the carcass. "Came right through the fence, like it owned the place. I shouted, but it didn't flinch. Just kept coming."

Dan had already started walking toward the bison, cutting across the field without a word.

The rancher watched him go. "That one doesn't talk much?"

Wyatt gave a faint smile. "When he does, it usually counts."

Dan crouched beside the bison. The body was still intact, no sign of field dressing. Flies had begun to gather, but the eyes hadn't clouded over yet.

He reached out, fingers resting just behind the shoulder. The hide was still warm.

He didn't speak.

Behind him, Wyatt kept the questions moving.

"You said it broke the fence?"

"Right through it," the rancher said. "Wires snapped like thread. Must've weighed a ton."

"Did you get pictures?"

"I didn't think I needed to. Thought I was calling folks who understood this stuff."

Dan stood slowly, eyes still on the animal.

"You shot it in the field?" he asked, voice flat.

The rancher turned. "It was on *my* land."

Dan took a step forward, not aggressive, just closer.

"You shot it for being where it's always been," he said. "You just happened to build something in its path."

The rancher bristled. "D'you got a problem with how I protect my property?"

Dan stared at him. "Yeah. I do."

The rancher didn't move, but his stance tightened—boots planted a little wider, chin angling up just slightly.

Wyatt stepped in, voice even. "Let's all take a breath here."

Dan didn't look at him. His eyes were still on the man across from him—measuring him against a longer scale.

The wind bent the grass into slow waves. A single crow called once from somewhere behind the tree line and was silent.

The rancher broke first. "Look, I'm not out here trying to start something. I've lost enough pasture to these damn things. If it was cattle crossing into the park, I'd be getting fined. But when it's one of yours I'm supposed to just stand here and let it wreck my land?"

Dan finally turned to look at him fully.

"It didn't wreck anything," he said. "It walked. That's what they do. That's what they've always done."

The rancher let out a short, bitter laugh. "You talk like it was sacred. It's a cow in a shaggy coat."

Dan took another step forward.

"No," he said. "It was a bison. And you killed it because you couldn't see the difference."

The rancher squared his shoulders. "I've got a right to protect what's mine."

Dan didn't stop.

"You think owning land gives you the right to kill whatever crosses it?" His voice was quiet and steady. "You think a fence draws some kind of sacred line between you and everything else? You're not protecting anything. You're just afraid of what you can't control."

The man took a step back, not much, but enough. "What the hell are you even talking about?"

Dan kept coming.

"You killed something you don't understand," he said. "Something older than every mile of wire in this valley. You didn't act in self-defense. You acted in fear."

The rancher's face went red. "Are you threatening me, ranger?"

Wyatt stepped between them.

"Alright," he said, hand lightly against Dan's chest. "We're done."

Dan didn't move right away.

Wyatt's voice lowered. "Let's go."

Dan took a step back, turning, he walked toward the truck.

Wyatt gave the rancher a nod, just enough to end it, and followed.

Back in the truck, the doors shut with a hollow thud.

The land rolled past, fences on one side, open forest on the other.

Wyatt kept one hand on the wheel, the other resting on his thigh. He glanced over once, then again.

"You can't talk to people like that," he said finally.

Dan stared out the window.

"I didn't threaten him," he said.

"No," Wyatt agreed. "You didn't."

The road narrowed. A hawk lifted from a fence post as they passed.

After a long pause, Wyatt said, "You were right, though."

Dan didn't respond.

Wyatt added, "Still, there's a line. You cross it and it isn't always easy to come back."

Dan's hand rested on the doorframe. His knuckles were white.

"I know," he said quietly.

Later that evening, Dan walked Shankley out past the housing loop.

The dog walked ahead for a while, then circled back, as if checking on him.

Dan stopped near a shallow rise and crouched down, fingers brushing the dry earth. A beetle moved beneath the stalks. Out beyond the trees, a grouse called once, low and throaty.

He breathed in through his nose, slow and steady.

Shankley had moved up beside him and leaned gently into his leg.

As the last of the light drained from the sky, Dan rose and turned back toward the housing loop.

When he reached his door, he stepped inside and shut it gently behind him.

TWENTY-NINE

THE SCHOOL WAS EMPTY, but it still held a faint echo of movement—scuff marks on the tile, student artwork stretching down the vacant hallways.

Leona's classroom sat in the back corner of the building, cooler than the rest, shaded by an old spruce tree that brushed its needles against the window when the wind blew. The door stood open, and a box fan hummed on the sill, pushing warm air in lazy currents across the room.

Inside, Leona was arranging a stack of paperbacks by reading level—titles she knew by heart, covers worn from years of passing hands. Star was helping.

She moved with quiet purpose, taping up a laminated poster near the whiteboard. The edges curled where the old tape had dried out. Leona glanced up from her crate of books and watched as Star pressed the new tape down carefully with the edge of a ruler.

Leona sat back on her heels. "You're good at that."

Star gave a small shrug.

She crossed to the other side of the board and started on the next poster—an illustrated food web, wolves and elk and grass in a looping chain. Leona returned to her books, but her eyes kept flicking back.

Eventually, Leona stood and stretched. "Would you like something to drink?"

Star hesitated. Then nodded.

In the small staff fridge tucked behind her desk, Leona kept a pitcher of lemon water. She poured two cups and handed one over. Star took it with a murmured thanks and leaned back against a desk near the window.

For a while, they drank in silence.

Star placed her cup on the desk. "He's back."

The words weren't loud.

Leona didn't react right away. She swirled the lemon water once in her cup. "Steve?"

Star nodded.

Leona's voice stayed level. "Did he just get there?"

"It's been a couple of days."

Star looked out the window. The spruce branches shifted in the breeze.

"They've been drinking," she added. "A lot. I think there's other stuff, too."

Leona stayed where she was and let it come.

"Smells weird in there. Like bleach or something."

"What about you?" Leona asked.

"I just keep to my corner with the door shut."

Star picked up the cup and took another sip, "I'm fine. I just wanted to tell someone."

Leona nodded, slowly.

It wasn't the words. It was the way Star said them—flat, factual, like someone reporting the weather.

Leona crossed the room and picked up a stack of folders, then put them back down.

"Are you planning to head home soon?"

Star shrugged. "I left my bike leaning on the fence, I just have to grab it."

Leona nodded. Her fingers drummed once on the desk.

"Do you mind if I come with you?" she asked. "Just to check in."

Star hesitated. "I guess."

"Dan's around today. Would you be okay if I asked him to come too?"

"Yeah. That's okay."

Dan was on the backsteps, cutting firewood. The rounds were dry, splitting clean under the maul, and the rhythm had been steady enough to settle his mind. Shankley lay a few feet away in a patch of sun, one ear cocked toward the sound of the blade.

His phone buzzed on the railing. He let it go at first and kept splitting, but it buzzed again, a second time, then a third. He leaned the maul against the steps and picked it up.

Leona: *Star says Steve Gregory's back*

Leona: *Situation at the trailer sounds off*

Leona: *You home?*

He stared at the screen a moment longer than he needed to.

Dan recalled the name: Steve Gregory. He'd been drinking in the park, music blasting. Steve had been loud, half-slurred but ready to square off the moment they'd shown up. Candace glassy eyed on the tailgate, Steve's grin a little too sharp, his stare a little too long.

He exhaled slowly and typed back:

Dan: *Yeah. Home. Everything okay?*

The reply came fast:

Leona: *We're fine. I want to check on her place. Will you come with us?*

Dan glanced at the yard—split logs, low sun, a quiet stretch of afternoon.

Dan: *Why don't you both come here for a bit? Give it some space. Let things cool off*

Another text:

Leona: *I want to see the place. See what's going on there*

He rubbed at the back of his neck.

Dan: *I don't like you walking into that alone*

This time the reply took longer.

Leona: *I wouldn't be alone if you come*

Dan sighed and put the phone down on the steps. He looked over at Shankley, who was now sitting up, sensing it was time to move.

He gave the dog a dry look. "Guess we're going," he said.

Dan walked up to the Tacoma reaching for the door handle before changing his mind. "Let's take the work truck this time." Shankley had already drifted towards the Park vehicle and Dan shook his head. "Always one step ahead."

They pulled into the school parking lot just after four. A lone bike leaned against the chain-link fence near the side entrance.

He eased the truck into a space near the curb and shut it off. The engine ticked as it cooled. For a moment, he just sat there.

Shankley shifted in the passenger seat, ears up.

"All right," Dan muttered, and stepped out.

Leona and Star emerged a minute later, Star in front, she grabbed her bike and wheeled it toward the truck. Her face was tight and unreadable. Leona mouthed a wordless *thank you* to Dan.

He reached for the tailgate and dropped it with a practiced motion. "Let's get this in."

Star handed over the handlebars and helped lift the frame. The back tire squeaked as it rolled into the bed.

"Jump on in." he told her, voice low but not unfriendly.

Dan opened the door for her, and she climbed into the back beside Shankley. The dog gave her a sniff, then settled back down.

Leona got in on the passenger side.

Dan started the truck and they headed for Star's trailer.

Leona broke the silence first. "We're just going to check on things, make sure Candace is okay and that it's safe for Star."

Dan glanced at her. "I get it"

She nodded, eyes glancing in the rearview mirror to check on Star. She added under her breath "Steve. Alcohol and drugs. No food in the fridge. A girl trying to keep herself small." She shook her head. "I've seen it before."

Dan kept his gaze forward. "I understand. But walking in without a real reason—"

"We have a reason," she said, sharper than before. "Star said it smelled like bleach. We can't let this go."

Star had shifted slightly in her seat and was busy rubbing Shankley's ear.

Dan exhaled. "I'm not saying we shouldn't go. I'm just saying we don't have authority to do much. You know that."

"I'm not asking you to arrest anyone, Dan."

He shot her a look, then softened. "I know."

They drove the rest of the way in silence. The road narrowed, and the edges of town began to fray the closer they got to the trailer park.

A dirt track split the trailer park in two, a patchwork of single-wides—some newer, most dilapidated, peeling paint and abandoned cars parked at their sides. A few had lattice skirting and tidy steps. Others slumped into their plots, sagging under the weight of the years.

The truck slowed and the dust cloud trailing seemed to speed to catch them.

Dan scanned the lots. A large dog barked twice and went quiet. A TV played loudly through an open window. A middle-aged man stood in a sleeveless shirt beside a half-open shed, smoking as he watched them pass.

This was a place where people got left alone for a reason.

Dan glanced at Star. "Are you okay?" It was a question for everyone, but Star answered quickly.

"Yeah. I'm fine, you didn't need to come."

Dan pulled to a stop just short of Star's trailer. The siding was faded gray with a missing panel near the base. One of the front windows was cracked and patched with duct tape. Two folding chairs sat crooked in the dirt near the steps.

A second car was parked out front—an older model, windows tinted dark. The passenger door had a fresh dent.

"Is that Steve's car?" he asked Star.

She nodded once.

Dan didn't move. "Anyone else with him?"

"Sometimes," she said.

That gave Dan pause. He looked at Leona. "We're not walking into this blind. This could head south quickly."

Leona kept her voice even. "We'll be careful."

Dan unlatched his seatbelt but didn't open the door yet. He looked down at Shankley and placed a hand on his coat. "Stay here boy," he said calmly.

Dan reached for his sunglasses, then the small radio clipped to the dash. He wasn't planning on calling it in, but Wyatt was working today and he'd come if he could.

He got out and Leona stepped out close behind him. Star didn't move.

"Just wait a second," Dan told her. "Let us check how things look."

They started forward together, with no hurry in their steps, but every sense in Dan's body was awake, watching the windows and the door.

The trailer didn't look much different from last time they'd picked up Star to go to Martha's. A patch of grass that once passed for a yard was dead, hard-packed earth and cigarette butts.

From inside, music played—southern rock, the volume turned up.

Dan and Leona reached the bottom of the steps. He glanced at her, just a flick of understanding between them, then knocked twice against the aluminum doorframe.

There was no response, and Dan knocked again, louder this time.

The music dipped, then cut off entirely, and the screen door creaked open.

Steve Gregory filled the threshold, shoulders wide, eyes already narrowed. He wore a sleeveless tank, stained and stretched across his chest, and cargo shorts that hung low. A beer can in his left hand.

"What the hell's this?" he said.

Dan kept his posture loose. "Just checking in."

Steve's eyes flicked over to Leona, then back to Dan, and his lip curled into a half-smile. "Bringing backup now Ranger?"

Behind him, Candace appeared—barefoot, hair tangled, holding a half-empty bottle of soda. Her eyes were wide but unfocused.

Leona looked past him, just briefly, toward Candace. She stood arms folded, a dull gleam in her eyes.

"We heard from Star," Leona said evenly. "She seemed worried."

Steve snorted. "Star always thinks the sky's falling. The kid needs to toughen up." He turned back to Dan. "What is this, some kind of welfare check? You don't have a right to poke your nose in."

Dan didn't react. "You know how this goes. You keep it civil; we keep it civil."

Steve stepped out onto the top step, crowding the space. "You're on my property now, Ranger. You don't get to walk up here like you own the place."

Dan held his ground. "I'm not here for you Steve."

From behind him, Dan heard Shankley padding up—silent, tail low but alert. He'd slipped quickly down from the truck when Star opened the door.

Steve looked down. "What's this mutt doing here?"

Before Dan could say anything, Shankley inched forward, ears up, sensing the tension.

Steve lashed out suddenly with his boot—not a full kick, but a mean, sharp motion meant to send a message. His foot caught Shankley on the hindquarters, just above the leg.

The dog yelped and limped away, tail tucked, and before anyone could move, Star was there—shoulder down, hands out, shoving Steve in the chest with every ounce of instinct she had.

"Don't you touch him!" she shouted.

Steve took a half-step back, thrown off balance not by force, but by shock. His expression twisted—rage rising fast, and he swung.

Open palm.

Hard and fast.

A slap that connected with Star's cheek, sending her reeling away from the door. She didn't cry out, didn't fall, but her eyes went wide, like the world had suddenly tilted.

Dan moved.

He stepped forward and planted himself between them, steady as stone.

"That's enough," he said.

His voice was low, flat, words spoken with authority.

Steve froze.

Dan's shoulders squared, he didn't clench his fists. But something in him had closed, locked in.

"You just struck a minor," he said. "In front of a state officer. You want to keep going, go ahead. We can call it in, file a report, and we'll let the judge sort it out."

Steve's mouth worked, but no words came.

Behind him, Leona had moved to Star's side. She laid a hand gently on the girl's back, steadying her.

Candace hovered in the doorway—standing witness, silent.

Steve looked at Dan, then at Leona, then back at Dan, balancing, one foot in confrontation, the other in retreat.

He snorted, tossed his beer into the dirt, and turned back toward the trailer.

"This is bullshit," he muttered, disappearing inside. The door slammed behind him, a hollow metal snap that echoed across the lot.

Star stood still. A red welt was already marking her skin, but her eyes were clear. She didn't look at the trailer. She didn't look at Dan. Just stood with her arms at her sides, breathing.

Leona's voice was soft. "Come with me."

They stepped away from the porch together and back toward the truck.

Dan waited a second longer, scanning the window. No sign of Steve. No movement.

He looked again.

Candace.

She stood at the front window, barely visible through the smudged glass. Eyes watching from behind the thin curtain, her body shadowed and still.

Dan turned and followed the others to the truck.

Star climbed into the back seat without a word. Leona slid in beside her. Dan started the engine and pulled away. Shankley lay curled on the passenger seat, his head turned back toward Star.

They didn't look back.

Dan considered what had happened—how quickly it had turned, how just showing up had placed Star in more danger, not less.

He didn't regret going. But the outcome had been predictable.

Leona could give Star a place to sleep. But the world Star came from, that trailer, that man, it wasn't something you could rearrange into safety.

Dan thought of the Park.

Lines on a map. Signs and ordinances. Things could be protected.

But outside the boundary, a different path was in motion.

Ranchers poisoned coyotes. Developers chewed up winter range. Wolves blamed for cattle losses.

Leona was watching him.

"You're doing that thing again," she said.

"What thing?"

"Looking past it. Seeing the whole slope."

They turned off onto Leona's road, each breathing a sigh, thankful to be home.

Star opened the door and climbed out. Shankley followed her, stretching once before padding off toward the steps like he'd lived there all his life.

Leona didn't move. She sat with a hand on the door handle, the other resting loose in her lap. She looked at Dan.

"Do you want to come in?" she asked.

He shook his head. "Not tonight."

She watched him a moment longer. Searching. But whatever she saw, she couldn't name.

Dan touched her leg.

"Let Shankley stay with her," he said. "Just for tonight."

Leona nodded. "That's a good idea."

She stepped out and closed the door gently behind her.

Dan stayed there a while. Star and Shankley had already disappeared inside. Leona stood at the door, looking back once.

She gave him a nod, nothing dramatic. Just a still, steady acknowledgment.

Dan nodded back.

Then she turned and went in.

THIRTY

DAN DIDN'T SAY WHERE HE WAS GOING.

No call to Wyatt. No note for Leona. He filled his pack with what he always carried—water, knife, binoculars. Same weight. Same shape. But it felt different on his shoulders.

He drove. Just the feeling that he needed to go. Heading through the park.

Up ahead, a handful of vehicles lined the shoulder—doors open, hazards flashing. A small crowd had gathered in the tall grass near the ditch. Dan slowed instinctively and pulled over.

He stepped out.

A bear—a young one—lay half on the shoulder, half in the weeds. Its back legs were pinned at a sickening angle beneath the bulk of its own body, breath sawing in and out in ragged jerks. One paw dragged through the dirt, slow and useless. Blood soaked into the gravel.

A woman held her phone up, angling for a better shot. Another man crouched, filming in silence. No one moved closer. No one did anything.

Dan stood there for a moment, and an old feeling rose in him.

A scream.

From down deep.

From the hayfield. Something he'd always carried.

He turned and walked back to the truck.

Unlocked the case. Took the sidearm.

He returned without a word.

The crowd parted slightly. A few people stepped back. One man opened his mouth to speak but didn't.

Dan approached the bear. Its eyes tracked him, wide but dimming. The jaw moved once but made no sound.

He raised the weapon and fired once.

The shot cracked through the trees—sharp, final.

The bear stilled.

Dan lowered the gun. He looked at the bear—still now, almost peaceful. Stood a second longer. Then he turned and walked back to the truck.

He headed north until the road gave up pavement and turned to washboard gravel, the sort that blurred your vision and shook the steering wheel hard. He parked at an unmarked pullout and crossed into the trees.

No trail.

Moving without urgency, he let the terrain shape his pace, steep in places, soft in others. The forest was thicker here, older. Lodgepole and aspen mixing past and present, roots tangled beneath the earth.

He adjusted his pack and stopped, listening to the caw of a crow.

Dan walked for a while before thought returned, his mind drifting. He thought about Star. The way she'd confided in Leona, not in fear or anger, but in a flat resignation.

She wasn't warning anyone. Naming facts, then stepping back.

Dan kept walking.

After the slap. The way she hadn't looked back. And Candace, standing frozen, her eyes blank as her daughter walked away.

In the shade, the air smelled like wet bark—musky and fungal, rising where the rain had soaked the ground. It was the scent that always came before growth—or rot.

He closed his eyes.

The blue of Pitkin Lake.

He pressed his palm flat against the ground.

A buck's ears twitching. The scent of pine and blood.

The trees were dense here, limbs weaving in a canopy above him.

He walked without choosing a direction. The forest guiding his path.

He stepped over a fallen log, half-mossed, rich with the smell of decay. Beneath it, beetles scattered. A perfect world undone by his passing.

He moved again.

The air had weight to it—thick with scent.

He passed beneath a leaning pine, and something brushed his shoulder and he looked down.

A feather.

Black and iridescent. Crow or raven. It clung to his shirtsleeve a few steps before falling, soundless, to the forest floor.

Up ahead, another waited. Caught in a low branch, spinning slightly in the still air.

The forest watching.

The scent pervaded. Damp, warm and rising. The first breath of the world after the rain

He knew that smell.

It came before every shift.

A welcome.

His senses overwhelmed him—damp earth, pine sap, something sweet and faintly sour beneath it all.

He heard the crackle of the bark beetles. A low vibration in the ground—steady distant, water, or something moving.

The muscles in his shoulders tightened.

His fingers flexed, but the movement felt strange. Not clumsy, just unfamiliar. As though they no longer belonged entirely to him.

He looked down.

Still his hands.

But the proportions felt wrong. Their weight, the way they moved.

He crouched slowly and deliberately and pressed his palm into the earth again.

And he felt the earth press back.

THIRTY-ONE

DAN SANK LOWER INTO THE FOREST, knees folding, arms loose at his sides. His weight settled into the earth.

Into himself.

Trees stood close around him—sentinels.

A breath of wind moved across the canopy and touched him as he lay.

He felt his blood moving rhythmically—a tide deep inside. His pulse slowed—heavy and deliberate.

The forest was no longer distant; it lived within him.

Primordial.

Something that waited without need or name.

Dan exhaled, and the air tasted like fur and soil and bone.

His shoulders rolled forward, slow and heavy. The joints felt stronger.

His flesh broadened, skin thickened, and muscle strengthened.

The forest was language.

No before. No after.

He rose.

He moved.

Each step landing heavy and quiet. He could feel the weight of himself. The ground accepted it without complaint.

There was no trail. There was no destination.

A low-slung branch brushed his back. He felt the flex of the wood, the flick of needles against fur.

He passed a boulder cracked by time. Paused to sniff its edge. Something had marked it. Fox or marten.

Far beneath the surface of the soil, something moved. Tiny footfalls traveled through the pads of his feet, faint and steady like a heartbeat inside the earth.

Turning slowly, he rubbed his side against the bark of a tree—scraping off something loose, satisfying an itch he hadn't known was there. The bark bit into him, then flaked away.

The wind shifted.

He lifted his nose and tasted it.

Rain, distant. Pine. And faintly—ash.

There had been fire. The ground still remembered.

He was *inside* the world now, not standing on top of it.

He'd circled back toward the place he'd begun.

There was a pack at the base of a tree. Dusty. Slouched. Unimportant.

A jacket lay beside it, half-draped over a log, one sleeve caught in a cluster of ferns.

He sniffed at it once, then turned away.

He left no trail, only the faint divot of pawprints in the soft earth. Behind him, the clearing waited, holding its breath for someone who would not return.

Above the trees, a single crow circled once, then veered west, riding the last thermals of the day.

A dozen ladybugs moved quietly across the bark of a fallen log—red sparks with black spots, untouched by anything but the sun.

THIRTY-TWO

IT WAS DARK, BUT NOT EMPTY.

Warmth pulsed around her in waves—steady and alive.

She lay curled, massive and quiet, the long hold of winter cradling her in its stillness. The den was tight, close-walled and safe. Her body was heavy with sleep, but also with life. One cub nestled at her belly, another draped across her side, soft with breath and fur.

She could smell the earth and feel the memory of old leaves and packed snow above. The world beyond was frozen, unreachable.

The cubs stirred, tiny claws against her chest, soft sighs in the dark.

Outside, the mountain waited.

Inside, life curled tight.

Leona woke slowly from the familiar dream; the warmth of the den still wrapped around her like a second skin.

The winter light crept through her window, pale as morning began. Her breath rose in the cold air. Shankley lay curled at her feet, and somewhere outside a bird had begun a quiet call.

Leona lay there a moment longer, listening. Holding the dream gently in her chest, like truth.

Then she rose quietly, careful not to disturb Star.

Slipped on her boots.

And stepped outside into the waking world, Shankley on her heels.

"All things share the same breath—the beast, the tree, the man. The air shares its spirit with all the life it supports."

—attributed to Chief Seattle

Follow Timothy Hargreaves

Facebook:
@timothyhargreavesbooks
Goodreads:
https://www.goodreads.com/author/show/58453207.

www.timothyhargreaves.com

www.ingramcontent.com/pod-product-compliance
Lightning Source LLC
LaVergne TN
LVHW100516110826
845146LV00002B/665